# SINCE YOU'VE BEAN GONE

## A SECOND CHANCE ROMANCE

FARM 2 FORKING
BOOK 1

## LAINEY DAVIS

# ABOUT THE BOOK

Waking up hungover in the sheep pen is the least of my problems.

The worst? A foreclosure notice for my family farm.

Scratch that. The actual worst is the woman delivering the news: my ex, who broke my heart and left me behind for the big city.

I've spent a decade trying to forget Lia Thorne, and now she's the only one who can help my family dig ourselves out from our crushing debt and even stronger egos.

I'm not afraid to get my hands dirty. And if I go along with Lia's new-fangled scheme, maybe I can win back more than my finances …

Just as long as my meddling grandma and her spoiled sheep don't interfere.

*Since You've Bean Gone* kicks off the Farm 2 Forking crop of laugh out loud romantic comedies set on Bedd Fellows Farm.

**Dig into this swoony, unputdownable second-chance**

*romance by USA Today bestselling author Lainey Davis and buckle up for an un-baa-lievable ride.*

# CHAPTER 1
# ETHAN

I forgot to bring the sheep.

I scratch uncomfortably at my button-down shirt collar, unused to wearing clothes I have to keep clean, and stare at my brother Samuel, who glowers. "You had one job, Ethan."

I could punch him. I could kick him. I could explain that, actually, I had weeks' worth of jobs leading up to this moment, including hours of phone calls to cancel Grandad's accounts and prepping things for the spring planting. I could ask my brother why *he* didn't just go and get the damn merino sheep.

But I don't do any of those things. Instead, I silently walk out of the lawyer's office. I climb back into my dead grandfather's pickup, and drive home to fetch Gran's beloved Baabara Streisand.

Gran asked Grandad years ago to build a palace for her pet sheep. At least that's how I see the decked out shed stationed one foot from the front door to their home. Should I call it Gran's home now? Gran is alone after decades of marriage. Well. She's with my siblings temporarily.

I park the truck by the sheep shed and pray the little bugger cooperates. "Hey, Baabara," I whisper, trying my best to sound approachable. "Hey, girl, I'm just gonna pick you up, okay?"

I walk toward the cowering, pampered animal, currently munching organic Timothy hay Gran special orders from the Pacific Northwest. Not sure why she doesn't patronize a local farm or why we don't grow it ourselves right here in Fork Lick, but the fact of the matter is this sheep is spoiled. Too good for Catskills hay. Too good for a barn. Too muddy for me to be hauling around in my only suit.

Baabara looks me in the eye and flicks her tail. She stiffens, like she knows I'm about to lunge. "We have to go to town, girl." I try to exude calm and move slowly. I lean right. Baabara scoots left. "Shhh, come on, now." I take a few breaths and whip out my hand, but she's too fast for me. Her hooves kick up filth as she runs tight circles around my legs, smearing me with muck. "Damn it, Baabara!" She catches me behind the knees, and I surge forward, but her own tight laps are her undoing because I get an arm around her neck on my way down. "Ha! Got ya."

I growl as I heft Baabara into my arms, realizing I'm 32 years old and I don't even know how to clean an outfit like this. I shove Baabara into the back seat of the cab, knowing Granddad would roll in his grave if he saw me put Gran's pet menace in the bed of a pickup.

By the time I get back to the lawyer's office, my

siblings have all seen fit to show up and they all frown at me as I walk in, like I made the proceedings late on purpose. "I have the sheep," I snarl, tossing a glare at Samuel and easing my expression when I see Gran's watery smile and my sister Colleen, Samuel's twin, clutching Gran's hand.

Lionel, the only lawyer in Fork Lick, clears his throat and looks up at me from his Coke-bottle glasses. The horn-rimmed frames blend in with his dark brown skin and give him the appearance of wearing aviator goggles. Heck, he probably did fly planes with Amelia Earhart.

There are no more chairs, so I stand in the back of the cramped room with one hand on Baabara's head, the other trying to brush hay and dirt from my suit coat. "Thank you all for being here," Lionel says. "As you know, we've gathered to read the last will and testament of Eugene Bedd." Lionel licks his lips and I force myself not to stare at the white goo at the corners of his mouth. "First, to Eugene's beloved wife, Ethel, Eugene has left the farm-house and acre of land surrounding. He notes you were the love of his life, and he wants you to always know the comfort of your home and the land you shared together."

Gran whimpers and my brother Alexander leans across to squeeze her other hand. He drapes an arm around her shoulder and swallows, but his eyes are focused on a spot on the floor. Likely where Baabara has dropped a deuce.

Lionel glances at the sheep. "I know this is unusual, and I thank you for providing transportation to Baabara Streisand-Bedd. Eugene has bequeathed $5,000 toward Baabara's care and keeping, to include the services of a specialty groomer to shear Baabara twice a year and prepare the fleece for carding, spinning, and eventual knitting by Ethel." Gran sobs and buries her face in Colleen's shoulder. I glare at Alex, who reaches up to scratch his ear with the middle finger of his right hand.

At this point Lionel sets his papers down on his desk. He folds his thick hands and sighs. "Folks, I've known your family a long time. I'm truly sorry we lost Eugene so soon, especially given all that you've been through over the years."

I stifle a groan and cross my arms. "Out with it." Jackson and Alex glare at me and I roll my eyes. "Sorry. Lionel, please just be straight with us. What's in the will?"

Lionel coughs. "Well, as you can imagine, Eugene wanted to leave everything to you kids. He raised you as his own—along with you, Ethel, of course."

Gran dabs at her eyes with a hankie. I grind my teeth together, waiting for the other shoe to drop. Lionel leans back in his chair. "You all have tended this land for generations. Eugene specified that he knew you'd continue to steward the land as he had done."

"But?" Samuel leans forward in his chair, sparing a pat on the head for Baabara.

Lionel cringes. "I'm not sure if you're aware that in recent years, Eugene leveraged the farm heavily to secure loans for new equipment, supplies, and that sort of thing."

Gran nods. "I knew there were troubles."

Lionel smiles tightly. "The outstanding loans and mortgages on the property total over $750,000." Colleen gasps and Alexander's eyebrows fly up. I'm sure mine do the same. Lionel continues. "This debt will need to be addressed before the estate can fully transfer. We do have someone from the loan holder in New York City who has come up here to meet with you about your options. I'm afraid it's beyond the scope of what we can offer here at Fork Lick Legal Services."

My brother Jackson looks around and sputters. "You're telling me Bedd Fellows Farm owes almost a million to the bank and this is the first we're hearing of it?"

I narrow my eyes at my brother the rockstar. "What's a million bucks to you?"

Jackson whips his head toward me, looking aghast. "A lot, considering all my money is tied up in investments right now."

Before I can press the issue, Lionel smiles empathetically and continues. "I know this comes as a shock. Eugene always did try to keep his business private."

Alex glares at me. "You're the great and mighty heir. You're telling me you didn't take a single look at the finances while you were over there picking up the reins?"

"What's that supposed to mean?" I press off the wall so I'm standing upright...in a small pile of sheep droppings.

Alex rolls his eyes. "Come on, Ethan. We all know you did everything Grandad told you to. You seriously had no idea any of this was going on?"

"You're damned right I did what Grandad suggested. And no, I did not know about the finances because I've been a little busy tilling 500 acres of soybeans!"

"Boys, please." Gran slaps the wooden arms of her chair and we all shut up. "You sound like oil and vinegar, always separating. We need to blend together and figure this out. Lionel, I apologize for my grandsons losing their temper. You know I raised them better than that."

"Sorry, sir," Alexander offers and turns to Gran. "I'm just upset."

"Of course you are, baby." Gran pats his hand. "Lionel, where's this banker? What do we need to do next?"

Lionel smiles and opens the door for a woman, who slides into the crowded room. I sink back against the wall, feeling the blood rush out of my head at the sight of someone I spent the past decade trying to forget.

Samuel guffaws when he sees her. "Lia Thorne. What brings you back to town?"

She clasps her hands in front of her gray pencil skirt, looking perfectly at ease in her office attire, her dark hair tied back in a fancy-looking twist. "I'm a financial advisor with Burgess and Bowers. I'm here to work with your family to avoid foreclosure proceedings."

The oxygen leaves the room at her words, and everyone stares at her. Even Jackson wipes the smirk from his face as my high school sweetheart reveals she's in on the debt situation.

"You knew?" My voice is hoarse, like I've actually been screaming instead of just mentally shouting at the imaginary ants currently agitating my pants.

Lia has the decency to wince at that, but she nods. "I was of course not at liberty to discuss Eugene's private financial dealings as one of our clients but—"

"You knew we're about to lose the whole farm and you let us find out from Lionel, crammed in a tiny room with a merino sheep shitting on the low-pile carpet?"

Lia's eyes go wide, like she's only just realized I'm here, or maybe she's only just remembering how she left me after promising to love me forever. It was supposed to be me and her taking over the farm, at the helm, riding a John Deere off into our sunset together. "I'm sorry, Ethan."

"Unbelievable." This time nobody scolds me when I shout. I look around the room one final time, shake my head, and shoulder my way past Lia and out the door.

I don't care how they get the sheep home. I climb in Grandad's truck and drive away.

# CHAPTER 2
# LIA

THERE'S POOP ON MY SHOE.

It's been awhile since I've had poop on my shoe, but at least this time it's from a barnyard animal. Does Baabara count as a barnyard animal? My brother told me the Bedds were building her an enclosure near the house.

I shake my head. I shouldn't be wistfully recalling the Bedd family and their eccentricities. I'm here to talk about money. I try to discreetly clean my shoe on the edge of one of the folding chairs, but there's no hope for it. The chair or the shoe.

I direct my gaze toward Ethel, clutching hands with Colleen and looking red-faced and flustered. "I'm so sorry we're meeting again under these circumstances. I didn't get a chance to speak with you after the funeral."

She nods. "I saw you there, though, sweetheart."

I snuck in the back, like a coward, and didn't stay to talk to anyone afterward. I haven't ventured back to the Catskills much at all in the past decade. My brother and I see one another at our parents' senior living complex in Florida a few times a year, or when I can convince him to visit me. I cut ties with everyone else I knew in high school. I felt like I had to, in that moment, and now I never feel like I have the time to rekindle old friendships.

Today, surrounded by this grieving family I've known my whole life, I can't help but wish I'd at least sent some holiday cards. I close my eyes against the hallucination of an Ethan Bedd holiday card, him with one arm around a wife and the other around a child. Does he have the family he always longed for?

My hand lifts to the diamond bracelet around my wrist, a gift from the man who loves me now. Ethan would never have bought me anything like it. My life is also nothing like the one I might have had in Fork Lick.

Alexander Bedd coughs and I turn to face him as he asks, "So, what do we do now? About the money?"

"Right. Well, I think the first step is to move into the conference room where we have a bit more space."

Samuel snorts. "And a bit less sheep dung."

I nod my head. "That, too." I glance around the room. "Is there … a plan to get Baabara home?"

Ethel comes to her feet slowly, shaking her silvery head. "Ethan just needs a minute to cool off. He's like a custard that way. Has to settle before you can top him off with anything." She pats my arm as she approaches the door. "He'll come back for you."

A knot forms in my throat. "Excuse me?"

Ethel smiles. "The ewe. Baabara. He'll come back for her."

We carefully make our way into the conference room, such as it is. Burgess and Bowers arranged for me to rent an office here in Lionel's ancient Victorian home, originally converted by Lionel's father into the family's legal offices. Now Lionel lives upstairs, conducts business from the tiny room on the first floor, and set me up in what was surely once a library but is now a maze of filing cabinets, stacked paper, and other flammable hoardings.

I do like the big table with the old-timey green glass lamp, complete with pull chain. Unfortunately, I don't have chairs to offer the Bedd family and I stand in the door, tapping my lip and thinking about the best course of action. "I'm wondering if it makes more sense to regroup tomorrow? I can leave you with the forms from the bank to review and then I could come out to the house to discuss some potential options for you moving forward."

Ethel beams. "That sounds fine. It'll be Ethan you mostly need to convince anyway, and he's—"

"Yeah, yeah, he's setting like lemon curd." Alex interrupts his grandmother and struggles back into his coat. "You all do whatever you think is best. I gotta check on my dog."

He hustles out the door like his brother, leaving Samuel, Colleen, and Jackson to handle Ethel and the sheep on their own.

Colleen bites her lip. "Samuel and I rode in together with Gran."

Jackson shakes his head rapidly. "No way am I putting that sheep in my car. Do you know what this thing costs to have detailed?"

"Where are you getting a Bentley detailed in Fork Lick?" Samuel thrusts Baabara's collar at his brother. She must have wriggled out of it sometime between pooping on the floor and following us into the conference room. I glance over to see her nuzzling a stack of papers, yellowed with age. She begins to chomp as the remaining Bedd siblings argue.

In a frenzy of temper and wool coats, they all leave the house … and Baabara … behind. The sheep and I glance at one another. She continues to munch on the paper as I sink into my chair to wait for the predicted return of Ethan.

It takes him two hours to come back for the sheep. I hear the tread of his boots on the porch steps, and I know it's him without looking. It's unnerving to still be so aware of Ethan Bedd after so much time apart. I have no business knowing the rhythm of his stride, not anymore.

But, sure enough, he leans on the door jamb, looking much more at ease in boots and Dickies and a worn Carhartt jacket than he did in a suit. He looks damn fine, even in a tattered beanie. The years have been good to Ethan, which makes sense. He probably keeps fit working the land, just like he always wanted. I'm happy he has the life he wished for, although I suppose some of that is about to change.

"I came back for Baabara. Did she damage anything I should know about?" I shake my head and he snorts. "You could add it to my tab if she did." He clicks his tongue at the sheep, who looks up from her forty-year-old law journal hors d'oeuvres. "Come on, Babs. Let's get back in the truck."

She bleats at him in protest. "Since she's occupied for the moment, I wondered if you and I could talk?"

Ethan doesn't look at me, but squats down to snap his

fingers at the sheep. "You sent the papers home with Gran. We'll take it from here."

"That's not how this works, Ethan. Your family is in a very serious amount of debt. I'm trying to help you avoid foreclosure." He continues snapping his fingers and clicking his tongue at the sheep. "You stand to lose your land."

"I know what foreclosure means Lia! I may not have a fancy college degree, but I know that much."

"That's not what I meant. I know this is a shock to all of you, that your grandfather was operating at a loss for so—"

"Every farmer in these parts is operating at a loss. That's the way of it nowadays. We'll figure it out and get you your money. You have my word."

I rise from the chair and walk around the table, not daring to touch him but coming close enough that I'm hit with the wave of his scent. The memory had lain dormant for a decade…sweet hay and fresh air and Old Spice. And something special, something uniquely Ethan that drove me wild from the moment I understood what lust meant.

"Ethan." I wring my hands together at my waist. "The firm wants to foreclose immediately. I bought you some time by coming here. But they're ready to move swiftly and we need an action plan."

He finally rises to his full, impressive height. Ethan Bedd was a boy when I left for college. A large, strapping boy, but he's a man now, filled out and beautifully weathered, with a hint of stubble and a thick neck. The bulk of him shakes loose something powerful in my libido and I clench everything I can to stop the flood of desire I'm shocked to experience in his presence.

Who lusts after a grieving man, reeling in shock at the threat to his family's livelihood? When she has a doctor-boyfriend back home? Me. I do these things.

I walked away from Ethan and cut off all communication when I got my diagnosis my freshman year. And I'm finally in a relationship. I have a life laid out, and it doesn't include Fork Lick. I don't know why I volunteered to take on the Bedd portfolio. I certainly don't know what made me push the firm partners to let me come here in person to try and save the farm rather than foreclose and take the loss.

But here I am, with my job on the line and a devastatingly handsome ex-boyfriend currently sweet-talking a sheep.

Ethan meets my eye, his ice blue gaze shooting sparks as his jaw clenches. "And just what plan can we come up with that will satisfy these suits? You want me to pull a million dollars from the pole barn? Just leave us alone, Lia. You did it before."

I should follow him. I should defend myself or my work. But I crumple against the desk in his wake as Ethan scoops up the sheep and, once more, strides out of the office.

# CHAPTER 3
# ETHAN

I CAN'T TELL WHICH PISSES ME OFF MORE: FINDING OUT THE farm is in debt, finding out that Lia knew about it and didn't tell us, or having to sit with my arm around my Gran's prized sheep as I drive through town to pick up catalogs for seed we apparently can't afford.

Baabara follows behind me like a dog as I stalk through the Feed 'n Seed. Nobody bats an eye at her being in here, and I silently will her not to shit on the floor while I pick out the catalogs I need. I avoid eye contact with Chen at the counter and stomp back to my truck, shoving the catalogs in the glove box so Baabara doesn't eat them on the way home.

I drive faster than I ought to on the dirt lane, kicking up a cloud of dust that hangs in the dry February air. I pull off my hat and rake a hand through my hair. This is always the time of year Grandad worked on the books while I handled the machinery repairs and hauled beans to the granary over in Climax. I smack the hat against the steering wheel. If I'd gotten more involved in the books sooner, we wouldn't be in this situation.

I've always hated math, though. Never could stand it and happily paid my younger brothers to help me with my homework…which meant they did it for me while I took on their chores. Moving my body, working with soil, and fixing machines always made sense to me. I feel at home with a wrench in my hand. Sit me in front of a computer and I'm like a box turtle trying to cross a highway.

I climb out of the truck, whistle at Baabara, and open the gate to her palace. She doesn't move, so I growl and haul her into her damn home before stomping off to the barn. I have to lose myself in practical work or I'll destroy something.

Actually, that's an idea. Gran could always use more firewood. I switch directions, striding toward the stump where Bedd men have been splitting logs for generations. Grandad's axe leans against the trunk of an oak I dragged out of the ground a few weeks ago.

I quickly lose myself to the rhythm of the work. I split the wood into neat logs that won't be too heavy for Gran to pick up from the rack, not that she should have to do that with Jackson staying at the house. I snort because there's no way my rockstar brother is going to risk splinters moving wood. He'd have to switch to air guitar.

The light shifts and I'm sure hours have gone by before I stop to wipe the sweat from my brow. It's cold, even for February, but I lost my jacket and flannel a long time ago, working in just a thermal shirt as I try not to think about Lia Thorne.

We were just kids when we were together, and it's useless to pine after her all these years later. It's just that I always thought we were it.

She used to be what I daydreamed about while chopping wood, not the thought I try to escape. Lia was always college-bound but dreamt of coming back to Fork Lick afterward. We talked about making a life together—me working the land, her using her analytical mind for something big.

And babies.

Fire roars through the muscles in my back as I heave the axe, trying to drown out the future she and I aren't making a reality. That was a child's dream and I'm a man now, with man-sized problems. Like how to keep hold of this land, and everyone on it.

Once I've split nearly the entire tree, I realize I haven't had a drop of water in hours. I make my way up to Gran's house for a drink. It's quiet for a change, with everyone out at work or running errands. Sweat pours down my spine and chills my skin as I stand at the counter chugging glass after glass of water from the massive sink in Gran's kitchen. This is where she soaked beans for us, washed our cuts and, according to her, bathed us all as babies, and our dad before that.

Gran and Grandad gave everything they had to us kids when our parents died. They pushed through their own grief and took in five kids. Now Grandad's gone, too. There's no way in hell I'll let anyone take this home from Gran.

I already did my part to drive away Samuel and Alexander. Gran would never say so, but I see it in her eyes, the hurt I caused ignoring their ideas and bearing down on Alex just for being younger. Saving this place is going to require a lot more than creative accounting. Sweaty and sore, I have the clarity of mind now to see that

I'm going to need all my siblings' help to keep this dream alive. And that's going to require me to mend a lot of fences.

I set down my glass gently and reach for the flour sack towel to dry my hands and mouth where I slobbered a bit in my haste to hydrate. I spot a tidy stack of papers on the kitchen counter and lean closer to get a better look.

It's a stack of information from the bank, although I recognize Lia's handwriting in the margins. I trace a filthy fingertip along the fine print, noting my cracked and damaged nails in contrast to the white paper and tidy notes she made for my family. There's no getting around the massive red debt number in block font, but I do see that Lia has outlined a few options to start paying it down.

Chopping wood isn't going to solve this problem, and Lia's firm wouldn't have sent her if they didn't think they could get something out of us to put toward what we owe. I turn and tuck the towel neatly over the oven door handle where I found it and walk to the table, pulling out the captain's chair at the head..

I force myself to read Lia's notes from top to bottom, even if I don't understand much of it beyond the word "diversify." I take a deep breath and let it out slowly through my nose. I glance at the calendar Gran has hanging on the side of the fridge where it's always been. She made a note for tomorrow and circled it in pink marker:

*10AM. Lia visit.*

Next to the calendar is a photo of Grandad and me, leaning against the pole barn, filthy from loading beans into the grain truck last year. He must have known then about the trouble we were in, but you wouldn't know it from the expression on his face. He's smiling with his whole being, an arm around my shoulder, one hand pointing at the photographer. The whole thing is blurry, like the photographer didn't have enough time to wait for the lens to focus. That must have been early in Gran's smartphone phase. Now she's constantly taking videos of us to send to her knitting friends.

I feel a series of uncomfortable emotions—grief at the loss of the man who raised me, but also remorse at letting myself cling stubbornly to the principles of a man who, frankly, got us all into a heap of trouble and hid it from us rather than pulling us together like a team. Eugene Bedd clung to his beliefs in the best way to do things, and I took his word as gospel rather than listen to anyone else. Rigidity landed us in a hot mess.

There has to be a way to honor Grandad's legacy while making some changes that can reunite the Bedd family. Maybe it'll take Lia—an insider with years of outsider perspective—to show us the way.

I neaten the pile of papers, careful not to get them dirty, and leave them on the table. I can listen politely to what Lia Thorne has to say if it means saving Bedd Fellows Farm.

# CHAPTER 4
# LIA

As I toss and turn in my childhood bed, I can't seem to get the covers wrapped all the way around my adult body. I can't handle the light streaming in through the side of the curtain by 8 each morning, like a laser pointed directly at my eyeballs.

Eventually I give up on sleeping in and drag myself slowly, painfully out of bed. My condition comes with a fun bonus reel of symptoms like arthritis and stabbing abdominal pain, particularly in the morning. Thankfully, my brother gave me full rein of the hall bathroom for the duration of my stay, so I don't have to worry about crossing paths with him for my numerous and unpredictable urges to explode.

I down my meds and look around Asher's fridge for something I can eat that won't irritate the fragile, damaged lining of my digestive tract.

"I've got bean burritos in the freezer." Asher's voice appears behind me, and I shriek, slamming the fridge door shut and clutching at my chest.

"I didn't know you were up. I didn't hear you come in. Sorry." I bite my lip as I assess my brother. Loud noises typically upset him as much as beans tear up my guts.

He blinks a few times and shakes his head. "It's fine. I have a soft tread."

I laugh and glance at his slipper-clad feet. "You definitely do. And sorry again, but I can't enjoy your bean burritos. I have things to do today outside the bathroom."

Asher snorts out a "huh" sound and reaches past me to grab one of his frozen fart-makers, muttering his apology for forgetting about the beans. He pops his breakfast in the microwave and leans against the counter, arms crossed. "I take it you saw them, then?"

Asher and I grew up next-door to the Bedd family. Next-door feels like the wrong word, considering their property is a sprawling soybean farm and ours is just a few acres of trees. But nevertheless, theirs is the next-closest door to the house Asher now inhabits.

I nod, opening the fridge yet again and finding a few eggs I think I can scramble and cook in some olive oil. "Things are emotional, understandably. Ethan seems … reluctant to talk to me."

"Mm." Asher stares at the microwave and grabs the door handle just before it begins to beep, pulling out his breakfast without further comment. Asher used to be close with Ethan. I never asked if they kept in touch, but I also know Asher prefers his solitude. I don't think he actually leaves the house much at all.

"I'll be out of your hair as soon as I help them get situated." I didn't reveal any private financial information to my brother, but I did tell him my company sent me here to help manage the estate after Eugene passed. Asher either didn't care about the particulars or formed his own assumptions, because he never asked me for any details. I like to think he used up all his questions in the time it took to get me my diagnosis.

"You're not in my hair at all. This is your house, too." He leans a hip against the counter, chewing his burrito.

I frown at him. "You bought it from Mom and Dad when they moved. It's your house."

He rolls his eyes. "You're not some stranger off the street, Lia. It's nice having you here for a change."

I crack an egg into Asher's nonstick pan and listen to it crackle. "I never feel like I thank you enough, for how much you came to the city when I first got ..." My voice drifts off. We both know I had been getting sick long before I moved to New York, but we also both know my diagnosis came from the brilliant young doctor Asher always mistrusted.

My brother grunts around a mouthful of food. "Someone has to keep an eye on you. And your vitals."

I snap off the flame of the gas burner and glare at my brother. "You know Richard is perfectly qualified to monitor my numbers, Asher. Do you have to be like this? It's been years."

I brace myself for him to tell me a doctor should never, ever become romantically involved with his patient. Again. But he just sighs. "Stay as long as you need to, sis." He drops the burrito wrapper into his trashcan and wipes his hands on a towel. Almost like an afterthought, he leans in for a stiff hug—more of a pat—before walking into his cave-like office. He'll be in there building top-secret websites long after I get back from my day's work.

I decide to walk over to the Bedds' house, enjoying the sunshine on my face. The winter air is much less aggressive here without the wind whipping up the length of Manhattan. The tall buildings always seem to create a vortex of icy breeze that stabs right to the painful points of all my joints. Here, I'm able to stroll through the trees and frosty fields comfortably with just a coat and gloves to keep me warm.

I tap on the kitchen door after waving at Baabara, out in her tiny garden, and I smile when Ethel shouts for me to come on in. The entire Bedd crew is seated around the kitchen table, finishing an impressive breakfast for a weekday. "Come and sit, dear," Ethel coos. "Don't be shy about fixing a plate."

A glance around the table tells me there's nothing here I can safely consume, so I smile and pat my stomach as I hang my coat on a peg inside the door. "Asher fed me, thank you. He sends his love."

Samuel puffs out a laugh. "I'm sure he phrased it just like that, too."

Alexander elbows his brother. "You send our love right on back. Please say it exactly like that and record Asher's face when you do." Everyone knows my brother is gruff, but of course he loves the Bedd family, just like I know they love him. And they used to love me. Fork Lick is like that when you're from here.

I take the empty seat at the table, next to Ethel, and brave a glance at Ethan. I expect more of yesterday's ice blue rage, but I'm surprised when his face appears calm, expectant. I tuck my hair behind my ears and reach for my bag, where I have an identical set of papers to what I left with them yesterday. "So, uh, should we just dive in?"

Colleen nods and the boys—men—I need to get used to them all being grown now—grunt into the remains of their coffee mugs. Ethan surprises me yet again, saying, "please do." He rests his hands on the edge of the table, and I stare at them, at the strong fingers and prominent veins. I can see the calluses on his fingers where his hands have adapted to frequent friction and pressure. I remember how gentle those hands were, and I find myself wondering how the thick, resilient skin would feel now.

It is not okay that I'm having these thoughts. For so many reasons. I cough to hide my distraction and open my folder.

"I thought it could be useful to summarize how we got to this point. Eugene began seeking loans with my firm about five years ago when seed and fertilizer expenses increased more than the price of the crops." The Bedd siblings shift uncomfortably as I outline recent trends in the area where soybean farmers have been shipping their crops by rail to New Jersey and then onward to Europe and Asia. "Eugene's expenses continued to rise without any increase in revenue."

I pause to see how they're handling the information. A look around the table shows a lot of stoic nods and clenched jaws, but Ethan continues to look right at me, intensely studying my face almost like he's waiting for me to tell him how to feel about what I'm saying. I lick my lips and take a sip of water from a glass I'm not entirely sure is mine.

"I have a few ideas to map out with you. For starters,

there's been a lot of research about exploiting new markets and crops. Hemp, for example, has shown a lot of promise in—"

"Hey, now you're speaking my language." Samuel's face brightens at the mention of the versatile crop, but Ethan growls.

"Absolutely not. We are a soybean farm. Bedd Fellows Farm has always been a soybean farm. We are not getting into that hemp shit. Sorry, Gran."

Ethel waves a hand at him and then gestures for me to continue. "Okay, so that was just one of the options. I've also got contacts with a few exciting startup companies using soybeans for biodiesel and construction materials."

Samuel sighs. "If you really need to stick with soy, there are good options. New York City uses biodiesel in the city's fleet *and* switched to soy-based tires for the city-owned cars and trucks. Not that anyone cares about my opinion."

I nod, smiling tightly. "Many of our clients are investing heavily in these companies. I really think you could make a lot of headway with some local partner businesses."

"Local?" Ethan crosses his arms, his expression skeptical.

My phone buzzes in my pocket and I glance down to see an incoming text from Richard. I quickly thumb the screen to put my phone in airplane mode and shrug at Ethan. "Well, domestic anyway. Some as close as Ithaca." I pull out a fact sheet describing an in-state granary that's producing soybean oil. "Selling the next year's crop yield to one of these types of companies would be more profitable for you and make you eligible for state and federal grants supporting sustainable farming practices."

Samuel frowns. "Can I take a look at those papers about the grants? I'm wary about a few things." Ethan emits a low grumble. Samuel adds, "Half the time these projects are pork barrel ideas that get cut the minute a different politician is in office." I can tell Ethan wants to flip the table over at the thought of changing anything at all. I can feel the tension between the brothers seeping from their pores. I dearly wish Eugene had at least told the family a little about what was going on, so this hadn't come as a shock for them all at once. I start to see how the idea of changing anything about the business feels like they're turning their backs on Eugene...but it's not my place to point out that he didn't do them any favors leaving them in the dark.

"Even if we consider that—which I'm not—we're ten months from the next harvest and getting that income from a sale. What else you got?" Ethan looks like he hopes I have a purse full of magic beans to offer him, a solution that lets him keep things the way they are on the farm and somehow erases the mountains of debt threatening to toss them all out on their ears.

I sigh and flip to the final set of pages in my folder. "One thing we can do right away is apply for one of the governor's new grant programs." I hold up a colorful flyer about impact agriculture. "There is a program for farms looking to establish markets or food cooperatives, with even more funds for those supporting under-resourced communities."

Alexander and Jackson lean forward. "Grants sound like a good thing," Jackson says, reaching for the flyer.

I hand it to him and nod. "Yes. Definitely." I briefly wonder why a famous rockstar is bothering with all these legal hoops, but I figure if Jackson was going to cover the debt, they would have mentioned it by now.

Samuel frowns deeper and shakes his head, but Alex interrupts him. "That's like free money. We've gotten a few for Udderly Creamy in recent years." Ethan snorts at the mention of the dairy farm, which I'd heard from Lionel that Alex works for now. Alex ignores him and continues. "We had to use the money for the intended purposes, such as an energy audit or health checks for the cows." Alexander leans over his brother's shoulder to study the information. "But you guys don't grow food crops here."

I suck air through my teeth. "There is that."

Colleen taps her nails on the table and I glance over at her when I hear the sound. "How much food would we need to grow? Gran has her garden."

I perk up at this. "How big is your garden, Ethel? We can work with this."

Ethel stops clearing the table and waves a hand. "Just a little kitchen garden, dear. Nothing like you're talking about."

Colleen scoffs. "Gran. You're propagating–"

Ethel waves a spoon at Colleen. "Don't you have lessons to plan, dear?" She turns her spoon to the younger Bedd brothers. "And you three told me you'd turn the mattresses. Lia and Ethan should go someplace quieter where they can concentrate." Ethel starts cramming leftovers into old plastic food containers as if that settled the matter. "Why don't you two head into the diner for a nice lunch?"

I glance around the room, stunned that anyone could consider eating *more* food so soon, but I hear Ethan's stomach rumble. Or was that him growling at the thought of spending time alone with me?

# CHAPTER 5
# ETHAN

MY GRANDMOTHER IS UP TO SOMETHING. I DON'T KNOW WHY she's meddling and sending Lia and me out for lunch, but I don't like it. I do know it's hard to concentrate on the road when I'm driving Lia Thorne in my pickup truck, engulfed in the floral scent of her shampoo.

My body forgets the years that have passed since I was allowed to drape my arm around her shoulders in the cab, and I have to keep my right hand securely on the gear shift, so I don't mess up and invade her space.

"I appreciate the ride." Lia keeps her eyes straight ahead, same as me. She's got her hands folded in her lap, thumbs tapping against one another like she's as nervous as me about this situation.

"No sense taking two vehicles. How's that for sustainable practices?"

A tinkling laugh slips out of Lia's mouth and I turn to face her, just for a moment, seeing a smile light up her face. "Ethan Bedd, did you just make a joke?"

My mouth cocks into a half grin. "Now, why on earth would I do something like that?" Dang it, I am flirting with this woman. I need to knock that off. I school my features and keep my eyes on the road, reminding myself that she betrayed our trust as a family.

Except, the more I think about it, the more I see she was doing her duty and protecting Grandad's privacy, even though she knew he was making bad decisions. Maybe I need to redirect my frustration at Grandad, but that doesn't do anyone any good. The man is dead. I clear my throat. "It's nice that your company sent you for this. You know, instead of a stranger."

"I asked them to come. It's kind of a promotion for me…a trial run to see how much of the loan I can recoup. I've been sort of stuck in the same role the past few years. I've been worried they see me as expendable." Lia bites her lip, as if she realizes she basically told me she's using our family crisis to get a leg up at work. I'm back to my sour mood just as fast as I slipped into pleasantries.

"Well. Anyway, I'd rather talk to you about it than a stiff suit who's never held a newborn lamb."

From the corner of my eye, I see Lia smile again, a broad, glowing expression that shifts the energy in the truck cab. "That was such a cool night. Best part-time job I ever had. How many teenagers get to miss school because they were up helping the vet deliver twin sheepies?"

I snort. "You still calling 'em sheepies? Maybe you aren't the stiff in the suit after all." I turn into the gravel lot outside the diner, happy to see just a few cars there. I guess we'll beat the lunch rush and avoid too much gossip.

"I do wear a lot of power suits when I meet with clients." Lia has to shove her seatbelt buckle a few times to release the latch. I used to help her with that. It doesn't feel right to reach into her lap just now. She finally frees the buckle and hops out of the cab. I follow her up the steps to the diner, reaching past her to open the door for her.

I swallow a lump in my throat as she presses against me in order to fit through the door to the restaurant. I have no business thinking about how her ass feels through the fabric of my pants. Lia smiles her way through small talk with Latonya, who was a long-time employee here before I was even born.

Latonya sets us up in a booth near the back and I take the seat facing the door so that Lia is hidden by the back of the bench. I figure folks are less likely to approach me since they know I don't gab about weather or sports. They've all already said what there is to say about Grandad's passing.

I briefly wonder whether Lionel blabbed about the finances at all, but Latonya interrupts this train of thought by pouring me a cup of coffee before I can set my hand over the mug. "You're going to have me up all night, LT. You make it pretty strong."

"Well what good is weak coffee, Ethan Bedd?" She pats my shoulder. "I'll bring you the milk in a sec. You two know what you want?"

I open my mouth to tell her the usual—I always just get the special because I figure the cook thinks it's the best choice—but Lia says she needs a few minutes and Latonya walks off to wait on other patrons. "Hm." Lia was never one to fuss about her food before. But she's a city gal now. Woman. Lia is a city woman.

She frowns at the menu and sighs. "I'm not entirely sure there's anything here I can eat."

"What do you mean? Don't tell me you're doing one of

those kayto fads, or whatever it's called." I sip at my coffee, forgetting I haven't added the milk yet. I nearly spit out the bitter, viscous brew but I control myself and swallow it, setting the mug down and accidentally brushing Lia's hand with my knuckle. I snap my hand back like I've been burned.

She worries her lower lip and sets the laminated menu on the table. "I have some health stuff, and I feel better when I avoid certain foods."

"Health stuff? Which foods?" This is all news to me, both that Lia has something wrong, and that food can be a cause. Maybe she has allergies. I remember toward the end of high school when she had an upset stomach pretty regularly. But the doctors all told her it was just nerves about graduating and going away to school.

Lia waves a hand. "It's a lot of foods. Wheat, dairy…"

"Well, dairy's in just about everything around here at least." I tap my fingers on the table and smile when Latonya comes back with my tiny pitcher of milk. "Appreciate it," I tell her, pouring all of it into the mug to try and make the drink palatable.

"Yes, I know dairy is in everything. Hence why I don't think I can get anything here."

I frown at the menu. Half the lunch choices are sandwiches or pasta, so those are all out on account of the wheat. The salads here all have croutons. I continue to scour, unsure why I feel compelled to find something she can stomach. "What about the chicken nuggets?"

She shakes her head. "Breaded. Probably fried, too, which is also terrible for me. It's okay. I'm used to this." Lia smiles up at Latonya, who returns with her notepad in hand. "Can I have a double portion of the fruit cup?"

Latonya raises her dark brows until they disappear in her white curls. "Fruit cup in February isn't much to write home about. What about canned peaches instead?"

Lia beams. "That sounds perfect, thank you."

"Put a little cream on them for you?"

"No cream." I blurt this with an assertiveness that startles all three of us. I clear my throat. "She just wants it straight up, LT, thank you. I'll have the special."

"Special and peaches, both straight up. Got it." She winks and hustles away as Lia sips at her water.

I absolutely cannot focus on her pink lips around that straw, so I dive into the next worse topic of conversation. "So. You want to turn Bedd Fellows Farm into an organic vegetable operation?"

Lia shakes her head and pushes her water to the side. Her hand slips to a bracelet around her wrist and she starts absentmindedly fiddling with the diamonds. Hmm. "Nope. I have an idea and I want you to listen to the whole thing before you snort, growl, or slap the table."

I gesture for her to continue, even as I have to grit my teeth at the thought of making big changes to my grandfather's legacy operation.

"Hear me out, Ethan. Strawberries."

"Strawberries?"

She nods. "They need a lot of nitrogen, which you have in spades from years of soybean growth. They like growing near legumes, so they won't mind the rest of the farm sprouting up around the beds. And they're an early crop, so you can harvest in spring to get an influx of cash."

"Strawberries." I blink at her. I have never grown a strawberry in my life. What does Lia know about growing them? They strike me as too delicate. And how in the hell do you transport them? We don't have infrastructure for any of that.

Lia nods again and takes another sinful sip of water from that straw. "Mm hm. We'll have to plan a market on the property to meet the grant requirements, really bring in the community. I wonder if Colleen can bring her students for a field trip and if that will count as a teaching facility..."

She fingers the bracelet again and catches me staring at it, and her hand flies to her purse. Lia rummages for a notebook, scribbling furiously while Latonya sets a bowl of peaches on her side of the table and a platter of meatloaf on mine.

"Did I hear you say Bedd Fellows is going to host a strawberry picking this year? I love that! My grandchildren love doing those kind of pick-your-own things. Always eat more than they carry out, but who can get mad about kids eating fresh fruit?"

Lia laughs, that tinkling sound again. It seems to come so naturally to her still, laughter. She makes a face at me that conveys *See? I told you so*, and says, "I totally agree, Latonya. We hope to share more information about picking opportunities real soon."

"You working with Ethan and Ethel and all the rest? That's so nice. I wondered why you came back to town after all this time."

Lia pokes at one of the canned peaches with her fork. "Sort of. I'm staying with my brother and yes, we'll be planning this event together."

Latonya pats the table. "That sounds real nice, Lia. And I'm glad Asher has someone staying with him. He and Ethan are both turning into hermits."

I whip my face toward hers. "I'm here, aren't I? I get out."

"Mm hm." Latonya walks away, muttering about grouchy old white boys and Lia laughs *again*.

I shove a forkful of meatloaf into my mouth, chew it too fast, and swallow it, necessitating another gulp of the too-strong coffee. "Strawberries," I say again once I've swallowed.

"I think we can get you clear of foreclosure with ten acres," she says, like it's nothing. "We've got til March before you'd plant."

"March? That's in a month."

She waves a hand. "Plenty of time! There are five of you, right? Plus, I'll be doing most of the paperwork for the grant application."

I slump back against the booth with a groan. Apparently, I have a month to pivot to an entirely new crop, learn about the required fertilizer and figure out which weed suppressant we need. Oh, and convince my siblings to help me do it.

# CHAPTER 6
# ETHAN

"You're such a shit-kicking clodhopper." My brother Alex throws a napkin at me along with the name calling.

Gran swats at my brother with a wooden spoon as she stirs a pot of chicken noodle soup on the stove. "Alexander Bedd, don't you use that language in my house. I'll wash your mouth out with soap." She's been cooking since our meeting with Lia earlier today. I'm sure she posted videos about it, too. I guess it's as good a distraction as anything else.

My brother takes issue with the strawberry plan, not because he doesn't like the idea per se, but because he's been suggesting diversification, along with Samuel, for years now. If I had to guess, and I do because we never discussed it, Alex took more issue with being ignored and silenced than he did with the specific ideas getting rejected.

I don't blame him for not sticking around a place where he felt no agency. Alex eventually gave up arguing with us and started working for another operation in town, but Samuel kept pecking at Granddad about different farming practices in between all his research projects at *farm college.*

That's what Gran calls Samuel's Ivy League academic program. I'm aware that agricultural science is a valid field of research. I'm also aware that I've been backing up my grandfather for a decade, ever since I fully committed to Bedd Fellows Farm being my life work. And I've played right along, essentially telling Alex to mind his business, and let the adults do the thinking.

I sigh. No wonder he's irritated any time he sees me.

Granddad raised us along with the soybeans, and I never wanted to stray from his vision for our land. How could I ever go against the man who took us in, postponed his own retirement? His plan kept this place alive. I can admit now that I should have listened to my brothers when they sensed a change in the wind. After all, there had to have been a time when Granddad did something new—he wasn't always exporting the crops to Asia. Or, at any rate, *his* father certainly wasn't always doing that.

Alex refuses to apologize, and I refuse to get riled up about him calling me names. I know what I am. I'm what I always set out to be—a man who takes care of his land and his family.

Our grandparents took us in after our parents died, but they were already getting up there in age at that point. I've always taken on more than a big brother role with the four of them. Nevertheless, I always imagined my family would look a little different at this point in my life.

My siblings are grown now, and I don't exactly have the wife and kids I thought I would by this point. I've got a grandmother to take care of, an elderly sheep to mind, and apparently a heap of debt to overcome.

"Now look," I state above the din. Only Colleen actually glances my way when I say that. Samuel and Jackson have devolved into shoving one another and Gran is getting more serious about swatting them with her spoon. Colleen follows my eye to the ruckus in the corner and she puts two fingers in her mouth, letting loose a whistle that has Alex's and Samuel's dogs barking from outside.

The room goes quiet. "Thank you, sis." She nods. "As I was saying, I know I haven't exactly been open to change before now. Obviously, there are some extenuating circumstances. I see that we need to make changes, and of the options on the table, I agree with Lia that adding in a strawberry crop seems like the best way forward."

Samuel sinks into a chair next to me, rubbing his shoulder from where he and Jack were fighting. "It really pisses me off that you're open to these ideas from Lia Thorne, who left you heartbroken and a hot mess, but when your own brothers pleaded with you to just convince Grandad to *listen* to us talk, you wouldn't intervene."

I look at my grandmother, who has ignored the mild cuss from Samuel as she dumps corn kernels into her soup pot. "I'm not going to apologize for that a third time, Samuel. I'm just asking if you are on board to help me prepare for a spring planting or if I need to hire out. With money we don't have."

"You want my help, or you want my labor?" Samuel glares. "Because I've got plenty of suggestions for growing strawberries as a cash crop. You could visit the Cooperative Extension any day of the week for a customized plan for how to proceed."

"I've got enough ideas coming at me from Lia. You know darn well I need the manpower."

"You want me to take a leave of absence from my own paid work to help you here? I have bills to pay too, jackass."

"Enough of that, Samuel Bedd!"

"Sorry, Gran."

The shouting resumes until Gran bangs a ladle against the pot and everyone files over to the stove for soup. It's hard to argue with a mouth full of homemade noodles and perfectly-flavored broth, so we eat in silence until we've made a significant dent in our dinner.

Finally, Colleen folds her napkin neatly and sets it on the table beside her empty bowl. She steeples her fingers and looks at me seriously. "Ethan, you know we are all on board to do what we can for the farm. Despite what we feel about your breakup with Lia, we know she's a professional whose opinion we can trust." She holds up a hand to silence an incoming argument from Alex, who continues angrily shoving soup into his face. "But." She points an index finger at me. "You need to decide the structure of this place going forward. If you're going to run the farm, you need to do that. You need a business plan, employees, a plan for seasonal hires, whatever. You're going to need to manage it like a business, or this will happen all over again."

She leans back in her seat and her words settle around the room. Gran grunts, which I interpret as her saying that our grandfather never made things like a business plan and only outsourced the bare minimum in terms of seasonal temps and number crunching. Which ... landed us here. Staring down a foreclosure notice before he's cold in the ground.

I'm not sure what to say to Colleen and my siblings. It takes me a long time to form my thoughts into words on a good day, and this one has been a hailstorm of emotions. Colleen waves a hand. "As you know, I'm a teacher, and I happen to be amazing at making lesson plans. I can volunteer to whip up a calendar and to-do lists for the strawberry stuff, but I need help knowing what the to-do items are and when they need to be done, and by whom."

"Whom." Jackson repeats this with a British accent and rolls his eyes.

"Whom," Samuel echoes, sticking his pinky finger out with an imaginary cup of tea.

"Whom," mutters Alex, tipping an imaginary top hat.

The callback from our childhood rolls over me with an ache. And then Jackson keeps on talking. "It's a farm. We know how to plant shit on a farm, Colleen. We've been doing it our whole lives."

"Okay, I'm out." She stands in a rush, her chair clattering against the wall behind her as she stalks toward the coat hook. She's gone before Gran can yell at her to stay and I hear the sound of her car spinning up gravel as she drives too fast down the lane toward town.

"Where do you think she's going?" Alex looks out the windows as if he can see her in the dark.

"No idea," I say. "But I'm glad she's actually leaving the house." I stand, more slowly and taking care with my chair, and start to gather empty bowls and spoons from the table. I'm looking forward to my own home down the lane a bit. It's more of a cabin, I suppose, but it's mine and I built it myself. Nobody goes in there. Nobody makes noise while I'm trying to think. Gran calls it my fortress of solitude. After an hour arguing with my siblings, I'm craving the feel of my own sheets.

My brothers each rise to help put away the food and wash up as Gran gets herself a cup of tea and settles into her rocking chair by the wood stove, knitting needles clacking. I smile at the neatly stacked logs I brought in. I like that she can use them to find comfort for herself amidst all this upheaval.

A few minutes later, I'm done washing bowls and ready to head out when Jackson stops me with a hand on my arm. "Stay for a night cap?"

I shake my head.

Sam and Alex are already back in their seats and Jackson stretches to the cupboard above the fridge, peering into the tiny space. "Found it." He pulls out the cheap, terrible whiskey that Grandad drank a few times a year. "Come on, Ethan. Let's toast to new ways of doing things." I hesitate, not wanting the particular brand of hangover that comes with cheap whiskey. Jackson rolls his eyes. "I'm flying home tomorrow. Hang out with me already."

Samuel's eyes bore into me. "I'm heading back to work tomorrow, too. You're on your own after this."

Alex shakes his head. "Nah. He's got Colleen here to help." I don't like how my brothers laugh at that remark, but I also don't open my mouth to stick up for her. I watch as each of my brothers takes a pull straight from the bottle. Less of a toast than a mournful, sloppy blitz if you ask me, which none of them did.

Jackson holds the bottle by the neck, shaking it at me. "To strawberries," he says. "Come on, Ethan."

I take the bottle from him and pour a sip into my mouth. It burns the hairs in my nose and I cough. I chase the whiskey with Samuel's glass of water. I should leave, but I sit down with my brothers. I'm trying to get along with them better. When they hand me the bottle again, I drink it slowly.

I stare at my brothers, who have basically become strangers, and I've had just enough whiskey to ask the question that's been burning in my belly since Lionel read the will. "Jackson." I press my palms to the table. "Why aren't you giving us the money?"

We all stare at him. The only sound in the kitchen is Gran's old clock ticking louder than ever as Jackson takes another pull from the whiskey bottle. "I would if I could. You have to know that." He wipes his mouth with the back of his hand and sighs. "I told you, I've got no liquidity. You have no idea…"

Samuel grunts. "You're right. We have no idea what it's like to have no money."

Alex throws a napkin at him and the three of them start chugging whiskey and calling each other names. By the time I remember that Jackson didn't really answer the question, I'm too drunk to make him elaborate.

# CHAPTER 7
# LIA

I NOW KNOW MORE ABOUT FARM GRANTS THAN I EVER imagined. I worked from home today ... well, Asher's home ... and researched absolutely everything I could about community agriculture and festivals and pick-your-own operations. Which is why I missed my appointment to get blood drawn at the lab over in Climax.

I wasn't sure how long I'd be back here in Fork Lick. Richard was really grouchy about me leaving the city to begin with and blew a gasket at the idea of me getting blood drawn at a lab outside his sphere of influence.

He upset me with his tone, actually, and I ignored his texts. I've also been putting off calling his office to discuss my options for my next medication infusion. But I can't even have that conversation without my blood draw. Shoot. There are definitely drawbacks sometimes to dating my doctor...

A knock at the door startles me from the nightmare that is this bloodwork scheduling app. I walk to the door muttering about terrible web interfaces, forgetting to wonder why someone would be knocking on Asher's rural, secluded door at night.

When I pull the door open a crack, Ethan Bedd nearly falls inside, but catches himself with a hand on my shoulder. The contact shocks the breath from me. His hand is warm and strong and the nearness of him sends my tummy fizzing faster than a bite of fried food. "Ethan?"

He saunters in the door and kicks it closed behind him before stooping to remove his boots. I bend toward him, sniffing. "What is that smell? Are you okay?"

I forget that we've spent 14 years apart, that it's probably strange to move straight to direct personal questions with an adult man I've been away from far longer than we were together. I sniff again. "Is that alcohol?"

"Old Crow." Ethan breathes into his palm and sniffs, laughing. "Foul stuff. Not sure how Grandad could stand it." Free from his boots, Ethan makes his way over to the couch and sinks into it, thighs spread wide, taking up all the oxygen in the entire room. His cheeks are pink from the cold, and he seems to have walked over here in just a flannel shirt and jeans.

"You must be freezing." I look around for a blanket to offer him, but Asher doesn't keep things like that lying around. I'm guessing Asher doesn't lounge on the couch too often and I know he doesn't entertain visitors. "Hm."

Ethan clasps his hands together behind his head. "If this was before, I'd tell you to come warm me up."

I swallow, feeling like I have an entire crop of strawberries stuck in my throat. I perch at the edge of the armchair furthest from Ethan, looking around and wondering if I should offer to make him tea. "Are you here for my brother?"

Ethan's eyes widen, and I can tell he's just now remembered that Asher exists. Ethan shakes his head. "Nope." He pops the p. It's cute. Or it would be cute if Ethan was someone I was allowed to think of that way. I gave up that right when I cut off all communication and, from what I've heard, broke his damn heart irreparably. I lick my lips, waiting. One thing I do know is that Ethan takes his time before speaking, and if I'm patient he will tell me why he's here. The problem is that I'm scared his reason for being here will destroy me emotionally.

"I need to know, Lia. What happened to you? Why'd you give us up? And whose diamonds have you got around your wrist?" He drops his hands from behind his head, sagging further into the couch but never taking those blue eyes off of my face. I am held in place by that gaze, the depth of his feelings evident on every part of his body.

I close my eyes, hoping I can ignore the latter question and prepare to repeat the line I gave him years ago once I found the strength and concentration to make a phone call. "We are in different places, Ethan. I live in New York City, and you live on the farm."

When I open my eyes, he's leaned forward, scooting to the end of the couch closest to me. His breath whispers across my hands, twisting together in my lap. "I came looking for you, you know. To the city."

I suck in a gasp. "You came to the city?"

He waves a hand. "I asked at the college. They said you weren't a student there. It was like you disappeared off the earth. Asher wouldn't tell me a damn thing." He hiccups. "Stopped talking to me at all, actually. Lost a friend and my future."

Ethan speaks so matter of factly about the impact of our breakup, about his belief that we were destined for forever rather than just high school sweethearts. I'm trembling in response to the evidence of the pain I caused, and I start shaking my head, unsure what to say. I relax into the chair. "I've been so sorry about hurting you, Ethan. But I didn't know what else to do."

How do I tell him that the stomach cramps and pains were incapacitating? That I had to take a leave of absence from school because, despite what the doctors all told me, the "anxiety" became bloody, endless diarrhea. That I lost forty pounds in a matter of months, unable to keep anything in. How do I tell my ex-boyfriend that it took bleeding ulcers in my asshole for any medical professionals to take me seriously?

I stare at Ethan through my tears, remembering the months of pain and daily visits from a home health nurse who had to pack the open wound on my butt. I could barely tolerate staying alive, let alone focus on a boyfriend who already had his hands full with his family farm.

A puff of laughter escapes my throat at the idea of Ethan pulling bloody gauze from my backside every morning in between sowing rows of beans. I tuck my hair behind my ears and take a deep breath, uncertain if he will even remember any of this in the morning when the whiskey metabolizes. "I have Crohn's disease. It's an autoimmune disorder and basically, my body attacks my intestines." He frowns and presses his lips together. "For the first few years after I was diagnosed, it was all I could do to get myself to and from my treatments and focus on school."

A tear runs down my cheek and Ethan reaches for my

face, but stops himself before he touches my skin. "You got sick, and you didn't tell me, Lia. How could you not trust me to take care of you?"

Ethan crosses his arms. "I would have waited for you, Lia. I would have helped you."

I throw my hands in the air. "When? During the harvest when you're in the fields 18 hours a day? In between tractor repairs? Ethan, you have commitments here and I absolutely could not leave the city where my specialists practice. Hell, a lot of the time I couldn't even leave my bed."

He shakes his head. "How the hell could you be so sick, and nobody here knew about it? Something like that doesn't just come on all of a sudden like a heart attack… you went to the doctors here. I took you …"

I nod my head. "I know you did, Ethan, and I know you were there when they all told me it was just nerves about leaving. And I *was* nervous about leaving you." A wave of pain shoots through my spine…not related to my illness, but the emotional heartache I still feel at the loss of what I thought was my forever. But people don't actually find their soulmate in high school. Ethan and I were always going to have an expiration date. "There are Crohn's specialists in New York. Doctors who study these specific conditions." *And I'm in a relationship with one of them.* I bite back that thought because it feels like the wrong time to mention it.

"Will they cure you?"

"No, Ethan. This is forever. It's part of me."

He sits back against the sofa, assessing me with those eyes of his. "You don't look sick to me." He licks his lips and doesn't add anything further, but I can feel the heat in his gaze.

I cross my arms over my chest. Now is not the time to explain invisible, chronic pain. "I've got a routine in place now. Medications. A list of foods that I can avoid to ward off most of the symptoms. Because of the medicine I take, I'm very susceptible to diseases. The common cold can send me to the hospital with pneumonia. And let's not get into how expensive it is to keep me alive."

I briefly remember Richard reminding me of that fact during one of our arguments about me leaving to come here. At the time I chalked it up to him not wanting to be without me for an indefinite length of time, but recently I've been ruminating on the implications of him emphasizing the difference in our incomes. Being home in Fork Lick has given me a lot of time to think about a lot of things.

Ethan's eyes bore into me. I watch his face as he takes in what I've told him and finally, after an eternity, he says, "I would have come to you. I would have left here and gone with you and been at your side."

I stand, my own eyes flaring with anger now. "How would that have worked, exactly? Would you have gone to college and sat inside at a desk every day? What would you do in a city for work? What would you do without your siblings nearby and without the ability to keep an eye on your grandparents? Tell me how that would have worked."

"I could have figured it out!" he yells. Ethan has never raises his voice, not with me, and the shock of it has me sinking back into my chair. His voice gets softer as he adds, "At least I would have fucking known what happened." Ethan tugs on his hair, leaving it standing up in wild tufts around his head. "It was like you died. Just like my fucking parents, Lia." His voice catches and I long to hold him, to comfort him. Ethan shakes his head, glassy eyes focused on mine. " My parents were here one minute and utterly gone the next. But it was worse with you because you wouldn't communicate with me and I knew you were out there somewhere, turning me away with no chance to make things right."

Now he flies to his feet, his chest heaving as he sucks in gulps of air and starts pacing the carpet. "You were my everything, Lia Thorne."

I stare up into Ethan's glare, silent. What is there to say? I was 18 and made a choice in the midst of a medical emergency. By the time my health was stable it had been more than a year since I'd communicated with him at all. I could tell him I hoped he'd move on by that point, but that's a lie. The truth is that if I never reached out, if I never asked about him or connected with him in any way, I'd never have to *know* if he moved on. I'd never have to see a photo of him getting married or holding the babies he always longed to father.

It was easier to shove him down as a memory of when life was simpler, and I was happier. It's not like I'm still unhappy. I have meaningful work and I'm with an amazing man who saves people's lives. There's not a day that goes by that I'm not grateful to Richard, that he listened to me and got me on the path to better health.

These thoughts swirl in my head so loudly I don't hear my brother emerge from his office-cave. "What the hell is going on out here?"

Ethan whips his head toward Asher and frowns at him.

He points an angry finger at my brother. "Fuck you for playing along with all this, Asher. You were my friend."

Ethan stomps toward the door and shoves his feet into his boots. He's out into the night before either Asher or I can say a word.

# CHAPTER 8
# ETHAN

"Wake up, shit head." Something itchy falls onto my face and I swat at it. "I mean that literally." The voice is persistent, followed by more itchy stuff.

I crack open one heavy eyelid to see my sister and Baabara, both staring at me intently. I take a minute to sense my surroundings. From the smell of things, I did not stumble into my own house last night after visiting Lia.

It would seem as though I tumbled drunkenly into Baabara's bungalow. And I fell asleep in the sheep dung. Colleen throws another handful of hay onto my head, and Baabara doesn't seem to care that her breakfast is scattered all over her human brother, as Gran sometimes calls me.

With a snort, my human sister tosses a handful of something green and fragrant onto my face and before I can brush it away, Baabara begins chomping it down, her tongue tickling my cheek and leaving a slimy, herbal residue.

I shriek and jump to my feet, brushing myself off. Baabara cares only for the herbs, and she kicks up on her hind legs to get the remnants of basil and mint from my filthy clothes. "Why the hell are you feeding her? Shouldn't you be at work?"

"First of all, it's Saturday." Colleen begins to pet Baabara. "Second, you slept in, and Gran was freaking out about Baabara starving to death out here all alone, so she sent me here to get the hay and offer comfort food."

I sniff again as Baabara finishes the last of the leafy greens. "Where did Gran get basil and mint this time of year?"

Colleen puts her hands on her hips and embodies a deep, mocking voice. "Thank you for handling my morning chores for me, Colleen. You're the best sister in the whole world and I appreciate you."

I groan. "Thank you for feeding her. But where'd you get...is that dill she's eating?"

Colleen flaps a hand around the bungalow as Baabara begins pooping. "Gran grows all that stuff. She's practically Whole Foods with her sprouts and micro green varieties."

I scratch my neck and peer out the window toward Gran's kitchen garden. From where I'm standing it all appears fallow and winterized, though I think I spot a few asparagus poking through the soil. "I don't see any mint or basil out there, Colleen."

My sister blinks at me like I'm the dumbest child to ever grace her classroom. "Ethan. Have you not been down to the basement recently?"

I frown and draw my head back. "What's in the basement?"

My sister throws her hands in the air and stomps back

toward the house, leaving me with Baabara to contemplate my pounding head and a throat that feels coated in Timothy hay.

I make my way to the kitchen and gingerly drink some water. This isn't my first experience with Grandad's Old Crow, but I sure thought I learned my lesson about it years ago.

I spy the basement door ajar and curiosity calls me over there. When I peer down the steps I'm met with bright lights and more heat than I would have expected from a dirt-floor cellar. Except...it's not a dirt floor anymore. Someone poured concrete and sealed the walls. Was it my brothers?

The laundry stuff is right where I remember, but the rest of the space is taken up by a giant plastic tent with bright lights and racks upon racks of potted plants. I see Gran inside the tent with a watering can, singing to a row of herbs. She's illuminated by grow lights like Taylor Swift on her Folklore album cover.

Gran spies me staring and smiles, stepping out of the tent. "Ethan, you're finally up I see. Help me lift that tray of seedlings?"

I silently hoist the tray to the rack where she points, feeling the humidity and heat of the tent. It's like I stepped into a hothouse. And maybe I have?

"What is all this, Gran? Where did you learn about all this stuff?"

Gran shrugs. "YouTube." She taps her lip and stares at the plants. "Do you think these lights are the right lumen for starting from seed? Maybe I'll adjust the timer and leave them on longer..."

"Lumen?" I can't think straight. I wonder if I'm still drunk from the cheap whiskey. Since when does my grandmother have a sophisticated garden operation cranking in her basement? What else don't I know about around here?

"Did you finally come to ask my advice about your strawberry adventure?" Gran smiles hopefully as she zips up the tent and makes her way to the utility sink to wash her hands. "Because I know a thing or two about a strawberry patch."

I didn't know, but I see now that I should have. "I'd love your advice on the soil pH. I was going to visit Diego at the Feed 'n Seed and ask for help."

Gran beckons for me to follow her upstairs, where she walks to the kitchen window and smiles. "There's what you need, pumpkin. Fresh from the source."

I follow her gaze and spy Baabara prancing around outside her little house. I can't tell if she's basking in the sun or posing because she knows we're staring. I note that Baabara's enclosure has more poop in it than it probably should, and I realize it's been awhile since I mucked her out. "Hm."

Gran nods. "Hm indeed. Now go shower, Ethan. You stink."

I stumble to my actual house this time and wash up, trying not to dwell on my scattered memories from last night. Lia telling me about being sick. Lia telling me she was so fucking sick she couldn't concentrate on staying in school, let alone maintain any sort of contact with the outside world. I drag a hand down my face and pull a hat over my wet hair. Now, it is time to focus on the work to be done.

I do recall Lia reminding me of my commitment to my work on Bedd Fellows Farm. She's not wrong about that.

It takes me a week to get the farm equipment up to code and place my orders for seed and supplies. Baabara continues building up her supply of fertilizer as Gran keeps her in basil snacks, but one sheep won't help me cover the ten acres I set aside.

I have a lot of hours to think about things as I'm outside grading the rock-hard ground. I chose the acreage closest to the barn for this experiment, mindful that hordes of outsiders will apparently be driving in to pick their own fruit. I don't want them trampling my bean plants while they search for berries.

I eventually realize that Colleen was right. I should've been making plans all along. Instead, I planted all my trust in my grandfather. I believed his word was bond, and Alex and Samuel are also right that I discouraged them from speaking up, refusing to rock the boat.

Just before Alex got his job at Udderly Creamy, him and Grandad fought like hell. I suppose I never wanted to get on his bad side the way my brothers had. Plus, I never really had my own ideas like they did. I just wanted to keep up the tradition, keep the farm growing, keep things steady.

I wonder why my siblings feel so confident in their new ideas…they grew up in the same family as me. Same dead parents. Same heavy-handed patriarch. Surely, they have the same lingering fear of what it means to be without him. What it means to change lanes.

Nothing feels stable right now. It's like I've been floating in a hot air balloon for decades and we've run out of fuel, and I have no idea which bags of ballast to toss where.

# CHAPTER 9
# ETHAN

We finally get a warm day—warm for February, anyway—I decide it's time I put Baabara to work. In a sense.

I grab a shovel and a wheelbarrow and head over to her domain to gather up a winter's worth of sheep dung to work into the new berry patch. Diego suggested I get some goat crap, too, but I'd have to call Alex for that and I'm not crossing that bridge just yet.

I'm unsurprised when Lia makes her way up the lane and rests her hands on the fence. Because of course the next time I see her after making a drunken fool of myself, I'm ankle deep in ungulate crap.

"Hey there." She doesn't look angry. Her tone suggests she's nervous, though. I plop a final load of shit in the barrow and exit the pen.

"Morning, Lia." I feel like I should take off my cap or something, especially with her dressed so nice. Dark jeans hug the curve of her hips, and I can see the crisp white collar of her blouse peeking out from the black wool coat she has on. I shouldn't want to peel her out of those work clothes, but damn it, I can barely rein myself in. Why is this look so attractive on her? She looks every bit the banker she became. If banker is even the right word.

"Can we talk?" She pats the bag around her shoulder. "I've got some paperwork stuff to go over with you."

I nod and squint at the main house. There's no way I can go in there after the work I've been doing this morning. Gran would have my hide if I dragged shit into her kitchen, even if it is Baabara's. "We can sit in my place if you don't mind walking a bit." She flicks her chin the smallest bit in assent, and I lead the way. Lia falls in step beside me, her sensible boots the lone indicator that she knows how to be on an active farm. I'm aware of every sway of my arm, careful not to let my hand brush against hers, worried that if I touch her, I'll burst into flames.

We reach my porch, and she steps into the boot brush without being told. I smile as she scrapes her soles clean and leans against my house to remove the boots before we head inside. And then I realize that Lia Thorne is going to be inside my house. Her scent is going to linger there. I'll see echoes of her everywhere, for months afterward. I'm sure of it.

I swallow the dread and point her toward my tiny table. "Let me turn the heat up quick."

She shakes her head. "Don't worry about it, Ethan." She pats the table. "Have a seat." And then she blushes. "I shouldn't boss you around in your own house. I'm sorry." Lia looks around, taking in the sparse cabin. I have what I need here, but not much else. A small heap of Baabara blankets, knit by Gran, is my closest thing to homey decorations. "When did your family have this built? I don't remember a cabin here before."

I shake my head. "It wasn't. I built it after high school." *After you left,* I don't tell her. When I was moping around so miserably that Grandad insisted I find a project to fill my empty hands and distract my troubled mind.

"You built it? Yourself?" Her eyes widen, taking in the building with new perspective.

I shrug. "I had help with the plumbing. And the electric. Never mess with electricity if you're not trained."

"Mm. Thanks for the tip." She sighs and pulls a stack of papers from her bag, placing them on the table between us. It's a tiny space, never meant for more than one. I have two chairs but only because Gran insisted I keep an extra in my home for a visitor. More often than not, that chair holds my feet when I put them up in the evening. I try not to think about how nice Lia looks sitting in it, sun streaming in the window and sparking the gold strands mixed into her dark hair.

"Right. So, am I correct that you've started work on the organic strawberries? I'm working on this grant application and need to ask some questions."

"There's no way in hell we're getting certified organic. Too expensive."

"Really?" She frowns at her forms.

"It would take years, Lia. They go over your land with a magnifying glass, basically. I never agreed to organic. Nope."

Lia bites her lip and scratches notes across the paper. "But you're not using pesticides?"

I shrug. "I have no specific plans to, not yet anyhow. We have to figure out if the plants will weather the spring rains first."

She asks me questions about the estimated yield. I tell

her where I plan to let visitors park their cars. She lists off a host of gadgets from point-of-sale machines to digital scales and I start to sweat despite the chilly temperature I keep inside my house. Finally noting my distress, Lia says, "We don't have to finish this today. We've got the shell of the budget and project narrative. This is good progress." She smiles and I forget everything I was just worked up about. How does her face transform like that, from perfect into supernaturally gorgeous?

One small curve of those rosy lips has me forgetting my name, forgetting the hard years. Just plain hard. I shift uncomfortably in my seat. "I should finish with Baabara's crap while the light is good."

Lia laughs. "I wondered what your plans were for all that. How will you spread the ... substance?"

I frown at her question. "With a shovel. I've only got a few wheelbarrows full of turds to go around. I still need to source something for the remaining acres."

"Can I help?" I don't respond at first because I'm certain I hallucinated her asking me if she could participate in spreading manure by hand. "Please? I'm sort of an expert on poop at this point, and I think it could help inspire me for the grant application."

"You don't need to beg me to spread shit, Lia." I look her over. "You're gonna need gloves, though." Beaming, she claps her hands and heads for the door, leaving her bag on my table and rummaging in her coat pocket for a pair of mittens. "Not that kind of gloves." I shake my head. "Come on."

We walk to the barn, where I get her outfitted in a leather apron--I have to help her tie it--and a pair of the smallest work gloves I can find. They must have been from when I was a kid, and I suppose I'm grateful Grandad never threw anything away. What are the chances Gran wouldn't have repurposed these into a fly swatter or something?

"I know I shouldn't treat this like an adventure, but it is, a little bit." Lia keeps pace with me as I push the wheelbarrow toward the new strawberry patch. "I feel better than I have in months."

"I'm glad you're feeling good."

Lia winces. "I hope that didn't come off like I'm celebrating your loss or something. I just meant that—"

"I know what you meant. And if being here helps your disease, or whatever you said it's called, then I'm glad for it. Here, you can shovel the first scoop."

I point to indicate the first row of soil we're going to fertilize, and Lia gleefully flings a shovelful of Baabara scat. "You have no idea how much time I spend thinking about poop."

"You're right." I shake the handles of the wheelbarrow to loosen up our load. "I have no idea."

"Well, it's a lot. You know, I always was a big pooper."

I laugh. "I do recall you were regular." I can't believe I'm standing in the sunshine spreading stool with the woman who broke my heart, talking about crap.

"A lot of days, all I do is think about, document, and discuss doodie. I'm serious." She rests a hand on her stomach, getting dirt on the apron I'm glad I gave her to protect her nice coat. "I know where every bathroom is all the time. It's like how a CIA agent always knows where the exits are. And I keep a poop journal. There's even an app for it."

I nod at this. "Farmers have that, too. I call it my dung

diary. You know, for the fertilizer…" I drift off because Lia is laughing so hard she drops the shovel.

"Dung diary! Oh, god, Ethan. I'm dying." She pulls off a glove and wipes at her eyes, where she's tearing up from laughing so hard. She laughs so long and so loud that I chuckle at the sight of her. And then I'm laughing, too.

And then she leans back to laugh harder and slips in a plop of Baabara BM and lands on her back in the mud. I freeze, wondering if she hurt herself or if she's horrified or if that was the final straw for Bedd Fellows Farm. But Lia laughs even harder, deep rattling guffaws.

I squat down beside her, plucking the shovel from her side and leaning it against the barrow. "You gonna make it?"

"I wasn't so sure there for a while, Ethan." Her words are punctuated by breathy, lingering laughs.

The sound of a car horn draws my attention toward the lane, and I hold a hand up to shield the sun, seeing Colleen's car. It must be late afternoon if she's heading home from school. She skids to a stop and slides down her window. "What in the hell are you two doing out here?" She peers up as much as the seatbelt will let her. "Is that poop?"

Lia and I start laughing all over again. I pull her to her feet as Colleen groans in disgust and speeds toward the house.

# CHAPTER 10
# LIA

I can't believe I just rolled around in actual shit with Ethan Bedd. I spend pretty much all my waking hours thinking about poop, hoping I don't poop at the wrong time, hoping I can poop when I need to ... it's exhausting. People think it's gross. I never, ever feel like I can just talk about Crohn's disease and Ethan just ... rolled with it.

Shit is clearly part of his daily life out here and I find that so freeing, so validating. There's not one person in my city life who I'd feel comfortable telling about my poop journal. I marvel again at how *real* everyone seems in Fork Lick. I'm glowing as we walk toward Ethan's house or ... maybe I'm glowing beneath the layers of filth. He crunches along the path with a happy smirk on his face and climbs his porch steps.

I halt when we arrive, not wanting to track all this into his home. Sure, I can scrape off my boots, but there's no way I'm going to sit on his furniture like this. I find myself wondering how he plans to avoid a muddy mess and, when he opens the door, I quickly imagine him stripping right inside it before crossing over to his bathroom to shower.

Nope. I should not think about Ethan Bedd in the shower. God, just looking at his throat above his shirt collar has me simmering with desire. I must not, cannot think about the ridge of muscles along his spine, all soapy and warm …

I tuck my hair behind my ears and unlace the apron he lent me, draping it over the railing on his porch. "If you could hand me my bag from in there, I can head home to shower. I think I have what I need to keep going on the grant application."

Ethan frowns. "I'm not afraid of a little mud if that's what you're worried about."

I puff out a noise I hope conveys a multitude of emotions. "Ethan. It's not mud. I reek."

He shrugs. "Nothing I haven't smelled before. You should be here when I'm spreading the store-bought manure."

Why is his grin warming my frozen insides? Why am I feeling all fluttery over a poop-centric conversation? I shiver a bit. I still feel nervous to fart around Richard, the stomach doctor, and here I am just yakking about doo-doo with Ethan. "I just really think I need a hot shower before I can focus on work." I immediately blush, having mentioned showering in front of Ethan, who I'm now picturing in the shower. Again.

He nods slowly and holds up an index finger. Ethan ducks inside and returns a moment later with my bag in one hand and the paperwork in the other. When he approaches to pass them over, I can see his chest expand and contract with his deep breaths. "Thank you," I whisper. I clear my throat so my words come out louder. "I had a really good day today."

He cracks a crooked grin and the sun glints off his eyes. With his face all rosy from working outside, he looks like a blue-eyed Apollo. He is all muscled and tall with a quiet stillness that comes from the constant, steady work of pulling the sun across the sky or the beans up through the soil in his case.

"Just let me know what else you need for the paperwork." Ethan leans against his porch rail, body relaxed in a way I haven't really seen in the few weeks I've been back here.

"Look at you coming around to the idea that change isn't scary."

His brows shoot up. "Change is terrifying, Lia. Everything about it feels wrong." He pulls his hat off his head and smooths his sweaty hair back with his palm. "But you make it seem possible."

I walk home floating at his compliment. Of course change is possible, but I suppose Ethan and his family have been operating in a place of protection and recovery from loss and trauma for so long that they can't imagine another way of being. I realize that's true of me as well. It's not like I love the work I'm doing in financial planning. Nobody wakes up one day envisioning a life spent trying to turn around poor investments. Absolutely nobody enjoys claiming assets from people whose dreams are crushed. Well, nobody I like spending time with at any rate.

I do appreciate that Burgess and Bowers have given me

the chance to work with the Bedd family to turn their loan around rather than foreclose. I certainly appreciate their generous healthcare plans and flexible policies that let me control my health as much as anyone can with my condition. But today, sitting down and talking through the story of this land, weaving a narrative for the grant application, imagining incorporating the community into the harvest … today was special.

Confident my brother won't exit his office-cave until well past dark, I strip to my undies inside the door and make my way to the shower. I use every drop of the hot water, letting the warmth sink into my bones. Only after I shove my clothes into the washer on a sanitize cycle do I check my messages.

I smile and put the one from Richard on speaker. His familiar voice sounds out of place here in Fork Lick, telling me he's calling me as my doctor this time. "We *finally* got your labs from that po-dunk clinic." I frown, wishing he wouldn't talk that way about my hometown. "Your white blood cell counts are high, babe. I swear I'm not just saying that to spend time with you sooner. You're going to need to come in for your infusion as soon as possible. I told you it was a bad idea for you to go there."

I feel the bottom slip out from my blissful day at the knowledge that my immune system is up in arms again, and it's only a matter of days before it'll start attacking my intestines. I also don't like how I feel after listening to Richard's message. There was nothing warm or complimentary there. He didn't ask how my project is going. I realize now that I want him to ask me about my life outside of Crohn's disease. Or at least make a joke about it.

Richard's tone and his blunt message echo in the house, a stark reminder that I really don't have a lot of control over my life—not for long.

# CHAPTER 11
# LIA

"Ash, are you up?" I don't want to bang on his door, but he did promise he'd take me to the Hudson station and I'd rather not have to catch a later train. "Asher!" He had two days' notice to get himself up to make sure he got me there in time. But he did tell me he had a software update to babysit last night.

I pound my fist a few times and I hear a groan from within his cave. He staggers to the door a moment later, prying it open and looking at me through one eye, puffy with sleep. "Ung?"

"Oh, Ash. We gotta go. You promised…"

He emits a growling sound and slaps his cheeks a few times. He nods his head and disappears inside his room, where I hear frantic shuffling and slamming sounds. Asher emerges a moment later dressed head to toe in black sweats, a black knit cap pulled down low over his hair, his bare feet shoved into a pair of black Crocs. "We can still make it," he grunts, pausing briefly in the kitchen to stare forlornly at the coffeemaker.

I hold up an insulated tumbler. "I've got you, boo."

Relief washes over his face as we open the back door and creak open the doors to his SUV. From down the lane I can see lights ablaze at Bedd Fellows. I smile, thinking of Ethan waking this early every day of his life to feed Baabara and prepare for a day of work so different from mine and Asher's. "You should have asked one of them to take you," Asher says, pointing through the trees to the big farmhouse, where I'm sure Ethel is scrambling a few dozen eggs for whichever Bedd children are still staying with her.

"They've got enough on their plate without driving me all over the place."

Asher nods and snaps on the radio. "Sure, you don't want me to take a peek at your numbers? Nobody plots datapoints like me, sis."

"Nobody except maybe the doctor with a degree in this stuff." I look at him in the gray light as the sun starts rising.

Asher grunts in response. I rest my head against the leather headrest and think about the past few years. I felt the furthest thing from beautiful after all the ulcers and weight loss and precarious bowels. How on earth could I feel sexy or desirable when I spent half my life in a bathroom? And then one day about a year ago, Richard touched my face during an appointment. He told me a new medication regimen would open exciting doors for me, and I cried in relief, and he brushed away a tear with his thumb.

I reported all of it to Asher, expecting him to be happy for me. Instead, he flew into monster big brother mode and has hated everything about my doctor-boyfriend ever since. It didn't seem to matter to Asher that Richard got approval from the medical board once he disclosed our relationship. My brother is just over-protective. We don't talk on the rest of the drive, listening to financial news. Asher stops outside the Hudson station, and I lean in to kiss his cheek before hustling off to catch the approaching train.

It's a nice, two-hour ride with plenty of leg room and WiFi, so I am fully caught up on all my work email and paperwork by the time I elbow my way through Penn Station and catch the subway to Richard's office.

I used to have to check in to the hospital for a half-day when I got my infusions, but now I can do it right in Richard's clinic. I hustle in the door and smile at Prachi at the desk. "Hey, Prach. I'm back!"

She smiles, her dark eyes crinkling at the corners as she rises to give me a hug. "Lia! Dr. Richard didn't tell us you were coming in today."

I frown. "Am I not on the schedule?"

Prachi waves a hand. "We always do you like a walk-in. It's a whole thing. You know."

I don't know, but I'll ask Richard about it later. Prachi leans down the hall and shouts to one of the nurses that I'm here for my infusion and soon I'm hugging Lynn and Javier as they usher me into a room full of reclining chairs. Richard's G.I. practice sees a lot of patients who need similar treatments to mine, and I wave at a few folks I don't recognize as they snooze by their IV poles. "Isn't Richard here?"

I strip off my warm layers and roll up my sleeve for

Javi, who cleans my arm and has the needle inserted before I even feel the pinch. "He said he'd pop in." Javi flashes me a wide smile while Lynn hangs the bag of medication on the hook above the chair. "You're an easy one, Lia. Best veins I'll see today."

I smile and reach for my headphones, telling myself that Richard is obviously busy. He's a specialist physician in high demand, and I wasn't supposed to be here for another few weeks. I drift into a relaxed state, listening to an audiobook about agriculture. When Richard finally rushes into the room, it takes longer than I expect for my heart to warm at the sight of him.

"Babe! Sorry I wasn't here to greet you. It's been hectic —we're up for an NIH grant." He leans in and plants a kiss on my cheek. I wonder if it's the medication that has me feeling the moisture of his kiss more than I'd like.

I reach for him with my unencumbered arm, and he squeezes my hand briefly before his pager buzzes in his pocket. "I have to run. Are you still coming in two weeks when you were scheduled? I thought we could get dinner then. I want to introduce you to Bajwa from Columbia."

"Oh. I really hadn't planned to be away from the project again so soon. I thought we'd spend time together tonight." I don't have to remind him I can't just go to restaurants at the last minute without checking out the menu. The stress of meeting a famous researcher would make the meal even more precarious for my guts. Richard is often frustrated when I can't join him for networking drinks or, if I do, that I end up spending the night in the bathroom.

But his voicemail made me think he was eager to spend some time together. I sigh. It's not like I can stick around the clinic until he has free time—I sublet my apartment for a month since it didn't make sense for it to sit empty when I could use the extra cash. I'm starting to feel like a fool for not communicating expectations clearly with Richard. I guess we were both thrown by my bloodwork.

Richard winces and shakes his head. "Aw, Lia. I'm sorry. I really thought you'd come back in two weeks. I have rounds tonight at Mt. Sinai." His pager buzzes again and he pokes at it without looking. "I really have to start writing it down when you're coming in to infuse."

I want to ask him about that, why I'm flying under the radar, but he spins around in a swirl of white lab coat, like he's going to leave the room. "Richard, wait." My words come out harsher than I intended, but it's not like I can chase after him.

He spins around. I glance beside me at the other patients in the room and beckon him to come closer. I whisper, "I feel like you're not prioritizing our relationship, and that's not working for me. Can we talk abou—"

He pats my hand. "Let's put all of that on hold until you're back in the city full time. Just focus on your health for now."

Before I can process his meaning, he swirls out of the room with a wave. I stare at the doorway, flabbergasted.

Every twenty minutes or so, Javi pops in to check on everyone in the chairs and, panicking at Richard's mysterious words, I beckon Javi over. "Hey," I ask him, pulling my earbuds out and silencing my audiobook. "Prachi said I'm not on the schedule? Something about paperwork?"

Javi shakes his head and taps on the bag of medication above my head. "Don't know what to tell you, chica. But I can say that you'll be out of here in about 15 minutes. Did I already say you have the best veins?"

I roll my eyes at him. "You did. And thanks for the speedy delivery."

After a visit to the clinic bathroom, because of course I need the bathroom, I look up the train schedule and message Asher to see if he can come get me today instead of tomorrow. I feel foolish and frustrated with Richard, totally confused that he didn't even tell me to hang out at his apartment so we could talk more about what he just said. I don't have time to worry about it for long before I'm back elbowing my way through the crowds to board the train, assuming Asher can pick me up and take me home.

Is it really my home? I pause at the thought of that word. I'm camped out in my childhood bedroom in a house that now belongs to my brother, so I can oversee the financial process and prevent foreclosure on my childhood boyfriend's farm. Nothing about this should feel homey or warm, and yet I can't stop smiling at the rare early March sunshine, thinking about Ethan starting to plant the strawberries in between his regularly scheduled soybean ventures.

Asher has yet to respond about coming to retrieve me, so I text him another reminder and then take advantage of the sunshine. I wander around Hudson, smiling at the fancy cheese shop and art gallery in the little town. There's nothing "po-dunk" about this place or Fork Lick, even if my hometown is smaller than this one.

I frown again, irritated with Richard for judging a place with different resources than the city. So many of the businesses here boast about their products coming fresh from local farms, local artisans. The shift to strawberries can be the beginning of a connected future for Ethan and his family if they let it.

And then, as if I conjured him into being, I see Ethan emerge from a hardware store that looks like it opened sometime around the start of the last century. His gaze is focused on a cardboard box he has tucked under one long, strong arm, and before I can understand my urge to do so, I shout his name from across the street.

Ethan halts in his tracks, squinting into the sun, and smiles when he sees me. I feel like I'm in an Aubrey Hepburn movie when he saunters over to my side of the street, grinning, and says, "Lia Thorne. What brings you here?"

I wave toward the train station. "I had some business back in the city today. Asher's picking me up."

Ethan flexes his free hand and I try not to stare at the bones. "Well, that seems foolish. I'm going back that way. Want to tell him you caught a ride?"

"I don't know if he'll check his phone once he's in work mode. I'd say he was only half likely to remember to come and get me to begin with."

Ethan chuckles as I text my brother that I found a ride home. There's that word again, home. Ethan sets his box on the seat beside him as I climb in, and then he frowns at the giant box. "Hang on. Let me get this in the back." Before I can protest, he climbs out and wedges the box in the tiny space behind the bench seat, which I'm assuming is pushed back as far as it can go to accommo-date his long legs. The box creaks as he tries to shove it in.

"I can hold it," I suggest, not sure if I actually can.

Whatever's in there seems heavy, based on his face turning red with strain.

Ethan shakes his head. "I'm not putting that anywhere near you. If I drive over a pothole it could decapitate you."

"I doubt it's that big of a risk. Weren't you going to put it next to you anyway?" My phone dings with a message from Asher:

k

That's it. Just one letter. I laugh at his predictability. Ethan gets the box behind his seat and climbs back up into the seat beside me. "What's in there anyway, that you couldn't get back in Fork Lick?"

"Fluted Coulter blade," he says, like I should know what that means. "Had to special order it after some of mine cracked."

"How does a ... Coulter blade ... get cracked?" I lean against the window as Ethan drives, trying hard not to stare at his hand on the ancient gear shift. I can see the tendons moving under his tanned skin, strong fingers casually working to put the truck in gear and ... I need to stop looking. It's a losing battle, since not staring at his hand means my eyes are on his face. My thoughts are not pure or reserved.

Ethan talks about the perils of tilling the soil with old equipment, and I relax into the seat, enjoying the calm confidence he exudes when he talks about farming. "But you aren't doing all that yet? Because it's too early in the year?"

He nods. "I typically spend the winter looking after all

our gear." He shrugs. "And apparently now learning all there is to know about berries."

"There are worse ways to spend a freeze." I let my head rest on the back of the seat. It smells like old leather and motor oil. Very different from the barely-used-new-car scent of my brother's vehicle. I, of course, don't drive in the city, so being in cars at all is a rarity for me.

Ethan's brother Jackson's voice starts crooning on the radio, and Ethan snaps it off with a harumph. I can certainly relate to sibling squabbles, and I don't mind the quiet.

The heat starts cranking in Ethan's truck as we drive in the sunshine, and I shrug out of my jacket, resting it on my lap.

"What the hell?" Ethan glances at my arm, his face twisted in concern.

I glance down, noticing the bandage in the crook of my elbow where my skin is still a bit yellow and green from last week's needle jab. "Oh. That's just from my doctor's office. I'll pull the gauze off when I can get home and change."

"They do that to you today? There's a bruise as big as one of Baabara's ears."

I sigh. "You'd think I'd stop bruising as easily after all this time. That's actually from my blood draw a bit ago." Ethan's face is stretched in every direction as his eyes fly wide and he bites his lip, clearly worried. "I told you I have Crohn's disease, and how my immune system attacks my body?" He nods, shifting gears and getting in the right lane so faster vehicles can pass him. I like that Ethan doesn't growl or grumble at them for being assholes. He just carries on at the speed his truck can go.

"I had my regular blood draw and things were a bit off, so I got my medication early. That's why I was in the city."

Ethan frowns. He's quiet for about a mile and it's really flipping hard not to make small talk while he works out what he wants to say. "So, you can get the bloodwork in Fork Lick but you have to go to the city for the medicine? How often, usually?"

I smile. "I had to drive to Climax for the bloodwork, but yes, I go to the city. I mean, I live in the city, so I just go to my doctor's office every six weeks or so for an infusion."

"That sounds serious."

I stare at him. "It is serious—the medication suppresses my immune system. But it's also routine for me. I don't know how to explain it. This is just part of my life." My stomach growls, punctuating my thoughts as Ethan makes the turn into the Fork Lick limits.

He pulls into my driveway—Asher's driveway—and puts the truck in park. "Is it safe for you to be here, helping us? Shouldn't you be closer to your medicine in case things get bad?"

I pat his hand and quickly withdraw from the contact. I barely feel it when I get stuck with needles, but touching Ethan Bedd is like gripping an electric fence. I'm surprised my hair isn't standing on end. This should be the time I tell him about Richard, how he's both my doctor and my future husband. But I don't tell him…because I'm not so sure it's still true, not after what Richard said today. I swallow. "There's a hospital not too far away. They can call my doctor, and he can get me sorted out pretty quickly. It's been a long time since I had a flare or a stomach emergency."

The organ in question gurgles again and Ethan nods. "You'd better get inside and feed yourself, from the sound of things."

I nod. "Thank you, Ethan, for the ride."

"Any time, Lia. I mean that."

His eyes bore into me, and I feel the truth of his words. I could ask him anything and he'd do his best to give it to me. I might not have realized that when I was a teenager in crippling pain. I can see it now, but I also know it's not fair of me to ask him for anything more meaningful than a ride home from the train station when my brother is AWOL.

I hurry into the kitchen and shove a quinoa bowl in the microwave before heading to the sink to scrub my arm. I'm prying off the medical tape when Asher makes his way into the room. "Was that Ethan's truck outside?"

I nod and give a final tug, pulling off the tape and gauze and smiling at the lack of blood on my arm. "He was in Hudson getting tractor parts."

Asher frowns but walks over to the microwave when it beeps and pulls out my bowl for me while I finish scrubbing my arm. He stirs my food for me while I dry my hands and I smile. "I, uh, guess I asked a lot of you when I said you couldn't tell Ethan I was sick." He presses his lips together. "I'm really sorry if I caused a rift between you. I know you used to be close."

Asher shrugs. "I was away at school anyway."

"But you came back. And Ethan says he hardly sees you."

Asher laughs. "I never see anyone, sis. I hate people."

"Yeah, yeah. Well thank you, anyway, for protecting

my privacy." He opens his mouth and I tack on, "even if you didn't agree with it at the time."

Asher nods and wraps me in a stiff hug before grabbing a package of processed food from the fridge and slinking back into his darkened office.

# CHAPTER 12
# ETHAN

I'D LIKE TO THINK I'M UNCOMFORTABLE IN THE LICK YOUR Fork diner because it's a nice day and I could be out planting instead ... but the truth is I'm antsy about this lunch meeting because I have to talk business with Lia, and I'm just not good about business.

In the fortnight since I gave her a ride, I haven't seen her but there's tons of evidence that she's been nearby. She's been leaving lists on my porch for me, with stuff like "check your email, for the love of god" and asking me about return on investment for specific brands of seed. I get all turned around with those details. I used to think Grandad was teaching me what I needed to know to run every aspect of Bedd Fellows Farm, but given our dire financial straits, I have my doubts.

So, I'm here, spinning my hat in my hands while I wait for Latonya to bring me another batch of coffee strong enough to put hair on her own chest. I'm early enough that I shouldn't be anxious for Lia to arrive. I wonder if she'll wear that diamond jewelry again, and who gave it to her. Definitely not Asher. Maybe her tastes totally changed over the years, and she bought it for herself. I don't like thinking about it, but I'm not about to ask her. It would be worse hearing her tell me she has a man back in the city.

The bell above the door rings and I can't help the smile that spreads across my face at the sight of her ... but it's short lived. Lia's skin is paler than usual, and she has dark smudges under her eyes. "You look awful," I blurt as she makes her way to the booth and sinks slowly into the red vinyl bench. She winces. "Sorry. That was rude. But, Lia, are you okay? You don't look it."

She shakes her head. "This is normal for me. I'm just feeling a little off. I think maybe I ate some dairy yesterday by accident. Maybe Asher put butter in the pan while I was cooking us dinner."

I frown. "You'd get this sick from eating a little butter? That's intense."

Lia sighs. "I have an intense condition, Ethan. I tried to tell you that."

I hold up my hands in surrender. "I'm sorry. It didn't sink in with just words, I guess. Is there anything I can do for you? Should we meet somewhere else?"

Her face brightens as Latonya arrives at our table. "Oh, you're here, honey. I can't wait to hear what you think of the soup."

I arch a brow and Lia grins. "I called ahead, and Latonya made some changes to the soup of the day."

"Chicken and rice instead of chicken noodle." Latonya squeezes Lia's shoulder. "I'll be right back with a big bowl for you."

"That was nice of them to adjust." I don't know that I ever considered asking anyone to change anything about a menu item in my life, but I'm glad Lia was able to make sure she could eat here safely. Her entire demeanor shifts when LT slides a bowl of steaming food in front of Lia, freshly diced carrots bobbing in the broth with chunks of chicken I believe came from the farm where Alex works now.

Lia moans with pleasure as she sips at her soup. "Mmm. Oh my god, this is exactly what I needed."

I take bites of my daily special–a chicken salad sandwich–watching Lia inhale her soup and trying not to dwell on the effect her small groans of delight have on my groin. Lia takes a few more bites and slides her bowl to the side. "Okay. So first of all, you need to start checking email once a day, Ethan. You just do. Your grandma says you don't even have a Wi-Fi router in your cabin…"

I roll my eyes. "I don't enjoy any of that. When I check my email there's more junk than substance. Who has time to sort through diet pills and opportunities to win millions of dollars in bitcoin?"

"Are there any teenagers in town? Because I can pay a teenager ten dollars to set up filters and solve this problem for you, Ethan. Come on."

I take a bite of my lunch and wait for her to continue. The sandwich is amazing and so fresh. I should tell my brother I'm enjoying the fruit of his labor. Maybe I'll do that later.

"Anyway, when you do check your email, you'll see some invitations to join project management software. You stop me if it feels like I'm talking down to you, but I'm going to assume we're starting at square one."

"I need a square zero for that stuff." I wipe my hands on my napkin and reach for the little notebook I keep in my pocket.

Lia shakes her head and clicks around on a shiny electronic tablet. "I took my best shot at mapping out the farm's cyclical tasks, when they need to be done, what's involved, and who is the point person."

"Well that last part's easy enough. I'm the only person…"

Lia nods. "That's going to change, especially as we get close to the strawberry harvest. For now, I put myself down for a lot of the goal setting and strategy tasks."

"Goals? You mean beyond 'grow a good crop and sell it at a good rate.'?"

We spend an hour going through what feels like an Intro to Business course. Modern farms get by with very few people, especially monoculture operations like Bedd Fellows Farm. But Lia insists we need to hire seasonal labor for the damn strawberry sales that we need to schedule to secure the community farming grant. People to manage and pay with money we don't have. At least with the pick-your-own setup we don't have to find people to harvest the actual fruit.

My stomach is tied up in knots and I don't know why other than this is a lot of change coming at me all at once. Lia does have a way of explaining it so it feels a bit less daunting, at least. "Is there any way to go into this gradually?" I scratch my neck, not holding much hope.

Lia pats my hand and I remember she's not wearing a ring on her left hand. Just that huge diamond glitter frosting on her wrist. *Maybe there's still hope for us.* I silence that thought as soon as it slithers into my head. I focus on the feel of her skin against mine instead, not that that's any better. Lia says, "The time for gradual was a few refinances ago, I'm afraid." She groans. "I didn't mean for that to sound disrespectful to Eugene. I will say, I wish I'd been aware that he was working with us. I would have discouraged him."

I bite the corner of my lip. "I was wondering if you knew he was borrowing that much and just never said anything."

"I would have done all I could to stop him, Ethan. I hope you know that. I just wasn't involved in this portfolio at all. I only happened to overhear a colleague discussing the situation and…" she shrugs. "I sort of begged my boss to let me try and turn this around. They were really ready to take the loss, foreclose, and move on."

"That doesn't sound like good business sense. How is that different from what Grandad did, taking a loss like that?"

Lia waves a hand. "Oh, they have formulas and prediction models for everything. I did manage to convince them that I could talk you all into the government grant applications, though. Those are sure bets if you can get them."

I furrow my brow and look at the notes I took. "But we aren't sure we'll get approved?"

"Not yet." Lia takes a bite of soup and pats her stomach. "I have confidence. Barring flood or insect infestation, I'd say we're on solid ground in that respect."

"You should knock on wood, Lia Thorne. You all but invited the plague of locusts."

She slides her empty soup bowl to the side and shoves a few bills on the check LT left for us. Lia assured me this is a business meeting and since our family is her client, she's supposed to pay. The company is the one paying, in fact. It eats at me, though, having her pay for my lunch while we're out together. I want to be the one paying for her, I realize. But it's no use wanting what I can't have.

Before I can ruminate further, my mouth forms the words, "Want to come over later and see something interesting?"

Her face brightens and I forget that it's a bad idea to pine for Lia Thorne. I forget that we're in dire financial troubles. All I want to do is show her our new invention.

# CHAPTER 13
# ETHAN

"WHERE DID YOU COME UP WITH THIS?" LIA STANDS IN THE barn gazing at my tractor with a rigged-up sled chained on the back.

I can't help but grin with pride at the contraption and I say, "This is 100% Ethel Bedd."

Gran is beside herself, all bundled in a heap of Baabara sweaters and scarves. She claps her hands. "I got to talking with Diego at the Feed 'n Seed about my own berry patch. He hooked me up with a gal from Coxsackie."

Lia blinks and her mouth forms an adorable *oh* as she shakes with laughter. "I'm sorry. I forgot we had a nearby town called Coxsackie. Please continue, Gran."

Gran nudges Lia with her elbow. "I got old Cranky Pants here to weave in a few upgrades to make the planting easier." Gran points at me. "Let's go, Ethan! We're burning daylight here."

Gran strides out of the barn toward the intended berry patch, leaving Lia gaping at our tractor toboggan. I beckon for her to climb up into the cab with me and she squeezes inside, her curves pressed against my body as I drive us slowly to the front field, all tilled and ready for the matted root plants I've had warming in the pole barn with Gran's guidance. There's not really room in here for two, and Lia has an arm draped around my shoulders. I can just barely feel the weight of her fingertips through my jacket, and I curse the thick material for doing its job, insulating me.

We reach the field and I shut the engine off, helping Lia down from the cab. She changed after lunch into muck boots and jeans. I smile thinking about how at home she looks out here with me. "The way it works is one of us sits on the sled with the box of plants. One of us drives really slow so the sled-rider can shove the plants in the ground. Whoever rides in the back will scoop the soil on top."

Lia shakes her head, laughing, arms extended. "This is incredible."

"I call back seat." Gran eases into the sled, clapping her hands against her thighs as she leans against the stadium seat I lashed to the sled for her lumbar support. "Lia, you're gonna be stickin' 'em in."

I can't help the whispered, "that's what she said," that slips from my mouth, but when I see the expansive smile on Lia's face I'm glad I made the lewd joke. I wink at her, knowing I shouldn't but caring less and less about *shouldn't* as I watch her bend over to pick up the box of strawberry plants.

Lia climbs onto the sled, sitting cross-legged, smiling intently, so I hop back up in the tractor and get started. I move as slowly as I can without stalling the engine and look back over my shoulder. Gran howls and hoots as she flings dirt on top of the seedlings. As I till the rows, Lia deftly settles the plants in the ground, tongue sticking out with concentration.

I stare at that moist, pink berry and want to taste her so bad I nearly run over my sister, who appears out of nowhere at the edge of the berry patch.

"You just get weirder and weirder, brother. What on earth is this?"

I cut the engine and Lia waves from the sled. "Come sit! We're planting the strawberries."

Gran pats the sled in between her and Lia, and my human sister rolls her eyes, laughs, and climbs aboard. They give me a thumbs up and I start moving again.

Soon, we've filled a few furrowed rows and the girls are all laughing and chatting like old friends. I make a slow, wide turn and watch them in my mirror, liking how natural this feels. Even though Lia's only been back a little over a month, it feels like she's part of the fabric of our farm.

Before I can decide what to do about that, Lia groans in pain and I cut the engine again. I stare in horror as she clutches her stomach, face ashen. I leap out of the tractor and rush over to her. By the time I make it back to the sled, she's doubled over in agony, shivering. She starts moaning and shaking and Colleen looks up at me, concerned.

I grab a bottle of water from the back of the tractor and offer it to Lia, who slumps onto her side on the sled, still shaking. "What do I do, Lia? How can I help you?"

She claws at her stomach and slaps away the bottle of water. Gran frowns deeply. "I think she needs to go to the hospital, Ethan."

Colleen nods. "You take her, and I'll call Asher and meet you there."

Lia seems really out of it when I scoop her into my arms and take off for the truck at a jog. I never thought I'd feel grateful to have chosen the closest field for this new endeavor, but now I'm glad we're just a few hundred yards from a safe escape. I get Lia hoisted up into the cab and fly into the driver's seat. I don't hear a peep from her until she grabs my arm.

"You need to pull over. Immediately." Lia is white as a sheet, and I screech to a halt at the side of the road. Before I can ask what's wrong, she flies out of the truck and into a crop of spring oats. I have a hunch she's losing her soup from the back end, and I look around the truck for something I can take her to clean up. I wish I had something soft to make her comfortable, but all I can find are some fast food napkins.

I gather them up and make my way to the edge of McGovern's field. "Lia, I've got some napkins here. I'm going to set them down for you and turn around to give you privacy."

Her voice is muffled and anguished from the grass. "Thank you. Oh god ... Ugh." I hesitate before going back to the truck, worried she might collapse. But soon she appears, walking slowly through the grass, tucking her hair behind her ears.

I hand her another bottle of water and she cleans her hands a bit. I don't wait for her to ask for help as I hoist her back into the truck.

Lia rummages in her bag and pulls out some wipes,

dabbing at her face and neck. "How far are we from the hospital?"

I glance at the sign as I turn onto the state road with better paving. "Fifteen minutes if I drive fast." I reach over to squeeze her thigh, hoping to comfort her. Her breath comes fast and shallow, and I speed into the parking lot of Climax General Hospital. Lia immediately hustles into the emergency department, where she beelines for the bathroom.

I pause at the triage desk to explain I brought in a woman with Crohn's disease, and she seems to be in terrible pain. The nurse frowns and clicks around on her computer, glancing up when Lia slumps over the desk. "You got your ID, honey? I can see if you're in our system…"

Lia fumbles, looking for her phone, and I reach into the pocket of her coat for her, procuring her device with a wallet attached to the back. "Here's her license and insurance card." I drape an arm around Lia's shoulders, hoping my internal warmth will ease her shivering.

It doesn't take long for us to get set up in a room with a bag of IV fluids pumping into Lia. She sinks into the bed and closes her eyes and when I reach for her hand, she squeezes it, holding me tight as she falls asleep.

# CHAPTER 14
# LIA

I'm vaguely aware that Ethan Bedd is next to my bed, holding my hand, and my brother is standing in the room, arms crossed, frowning like usual. I take my time opening my eyes—my lids feel so heavy. I'm not sure how much time has passed, but based on the stubble sprouting from Ethan's face, it's been hours.

"Hey." My voice is gravely, coarse. I must have been vomiting.

Asher tips his chin. Ethan's head snaps up and he squeezes my hand. "You're up. Ash, go grab the nurse and tell her Lia's up."

I'm surprised to see my brother obey this unexpected command without question, and soon he comes back to the room with a nurse and a doctor in tow.

"Ms. Thorne, I'm so glad you're awake. I'm the GI specialist here, Dr. Sanchez." The young woman smiles and extends her hand. I try to lift my arm and return the shake, but my limbs feel heavy and weak, encumbered by IV tubes. Dr. Sanchez reaches lower and gives me a quick pat. "I understand you're having a flare up."

I clear my throat and sip the water Ethan hands me. "Seems that way. Were you able to call my doctor? Richard Hammond?"

Dr. Sanchez frowns and looks at her tablet. "I don't have a note about that. Sanjay, can you set up a video call with Dr. Hammond if he's in our system?"

The nurse nods and steps into the hall.

Dr. Sanchez continues. "I gather you've been in severe abdominal pain. I also see that you're fatigued. Your brother mentioned you've had some stress with a new job assignment?"

I nod and Dr. Sanchez clicks around her tablet. "We can schedule you for some imaging to see if you've formed new ulcers we should be concerned about, and I'd like you to switch to a liquid diet for a week to give your bowels a rest."

Ethan looks horrified by this recommendation. "Liquid diet? How's she going to get enough calories?" I don't doubt he'd wither away from a similar recommendation given the way he spends his days doing physical labor.

I pat his arm, or I try to. "I'm used to this, Ethan. It's okay." I should have sensed this coming on a few days ago. I should have called Richard. I was so put off by our interaction at my infusion that I just ... ignored my body.

Dr. Sanchez looks between Ethan and Asher. "She will need a lot of support this week with daily activities. I'm guessing Ms. Thorne will continue to feel rather weak for some time."

Asher spears both hands into his hair. "I've got a product launch in twelve hours. I'm going to be on call for at least four days. Around the clock." I hate feeling like a burden to him. I hate feeling weak and a burden, period.

I open my mouth to insist the doctor call Richard, but I realize that he can't take the time to care for me, either. He'd recommend admission, because he wouldn't be able to take the time away from his patients or his research. Not if he's trying to land an NIH grant.

"She can stay with me." Ethan's words carry a finality. I stare at him, about to protest, unsure what I'd say.

"Pardon me." Sanjay, the nurse, comes back into the room. "Dr. Hammond's admin says he's unavailable to talk today but recommends increasing the JAK inhibitors."

Dr. Sanchez frowns deeply. She looks around the room and then back down at my chart. "Ms. Thorne, may I be frank?"

Asher pushes off the wall and walks closer to the bed. Ethan sits up straight and folds his hands in his lap. I nod.

"I have some serious questions about your medication regimen. Your recent labs indicate toxicity—"

I hold up a hand and cut her off. "I'm comfortable with my care in the city, thank you. Can you let me know what needs to happen for discharge?"

Asher's mouth drops open. "Lia, I want to hear her opinion."

I shake my head. "I've had years of second and third and fifth opinions. Richard is an expert in this field, and I trust his advice."

"I don't like that guy." Asher's nostrils flare and Ethan's brows shoot up. "I don't think it's right that he's dating a patient."

The room falls silent apart from the beeping on my IV pole. After a bit, Dr. Sanchez licks her lips and says, "Right. Well, I'm going to prescribe a course of steroids to manage the inflammation and I'll ask that you have a serious conversation about your long-term medication plan sooner than later."

She hands some notes to Sanjay and they both back out of the room, leaving me with two fuming men. I hear how my relationship must sound to Ethan, and for once I don't immediately snap to Richard's defense. Ethan glares at Asher. "What's this about a man you don't like? Is he messing around with Lia's meds?"

Asher shrugs. "I don't know what he's doing. I never liked him." He points at me. "I don't care if he saved you. The man's an asshole."

Ethan rubs a palm on his cheek. "And you're dating him? Your doctor?"

I wish I could tell him the truth … that I don't even know where I stand with Richard after my infusion and his cryptic, uncaring speech. I say, "It's complicated, " and absentmindedly reach for my wrist, but I remember that I was planting strawberries before I came here and left the diamond bracelet at home.

A thought occurs to me. "I understand if you'd rather I not stay with you, Ethan, considering—"

He holds up a hand. "I said I'd take care of you, and I meant it. I have plenty of space and my place is all one floor." I don't bother mentioning to him that he doesn't have a spare bedroom in his tiny cabin. I glance at Asher, who has to work, and think of Richard, who wouldn't make the time to talk to me even when another hospital employee called him.

*When someone shows you who they are, believe them.* My therapist's words echo in my head. I recall the days when I lost friends, lost contact with Ethan, had to take a leave of absence from my studies. My condition changed every interpersonal relationship I had and those words were a mantra for me to protect my emotional reserves.

At the time I thought Richard showed me he was an observant man, a caring person who saw what was really wrong and led me down the path to health. When he first asked me out, first kissed me, it felt thrilling. I felt special and seen.

Now, I watch as Ethan takes notes from Sanjay on how to puree soups and which brand of nutritional shake contains the most protein and calories. "And that one doesn't have dairy? She can't have dairy."

Here in this hospital, Ethan shows me that he knows how to listen and does what needs to be done to keep the people he cares about safe.

Ethan claps a big hand on my brother's shoulder. "Ash, I know you have to get back to it. Can you grab this stuff at the pharmacy and drop it at my place? I can wait here with Lia until her discharge comes through."

My brother nods and takes a photo of Ethan's shopping list. He plants a kiss on the top of my head. "We'll talk soon." I wave at him and stare some more at Ethan, who has no obligation to stay here … in fact, he has a lot of reasons to be back on his own property saving his own family from disaster.

He clicks around his ancient phone, clearly out of practice in sending text messages, but then he looks up at me and smiles broadly. "Colleen and Gran got Alex to come help them finish the last of the planting. He'll do those things for Colleen even if he'll tell me to piss up a rope."

"You and your siblings have some animosity …"

Ethan nods. "We'll work it out. I promised Gran I'd mend fences."

Once again, Ethan's word feels solid. I have no doubt that he will do as he says.

# CHAPTER 15
# ETHAN

Ethan. Your place is too small."

I'm beginning to regret coming over to ask Gran for some pointers to welcome Lia into my cabin while she recuperates. Seems like the easiest thing to do would be to relocate Asher to my place and I could look after her at theirs, but Asher says I don't have enough internet for his fancy computer crap.

"She can't be doing the stairs up and down, Gran." I hurry to grab the stock pot from the rack for her before she bops herself on the head. "And neither should you, probably."

She waves a hand. "Pish." Gesturing for the pot, she points to the largest burner on the stove and buries herself in the fridge, rooting around for ingredients. "I'm going to make a huge pot of chicken soup and puree it and then have Colleen bring it over. I don't trust you to balance the seasoning."

"I can get the soup, Gran. Colleen has work to do."

"Suit yourself." She closes the fridge and starts

whacking at a chicken carcass with a cleaver. Her hands fly through the work, hurling onions and carrots and celery at the stove. She pauses and puts her hands on her hips. "Do you think fresh herbs would be too much for her stomach? I've got the nicest parsley coming up downstairs…"

I shake my head. "No idea. I wrote down ginger and … turmeric."

"Oh, that's right. Well, head down to the cellar and help me get her some mint and chamomile. We'll make some tea, too."

I had no idea tea was something someone could *make*, but of course it's all plants. I see that I have a lot to learn about growing food. A lot more than I ever thought I'd care to learn. I follow Gran to her insane garden and try to follow instructions as I pick from among the plants in her tent.

"Let me just rinse these off."

I nod and watch as Gran grabs the handheld sprayer attached to the utility sink. She rinses dirt from the mint leaves and chamomile stems and an idea forms in my head. There might just be something nice I can do for Lia to make her more comfortable, considering the tight quarters.

I'm not sure why I feel so compelled to take care of her like this. Maybe it's because she thought I couldn't before.

*Maybe it's because I want her in my house, now and always.*

I clear my throat. "I'm going to head home with the tea. I'll come back for the soup in the morning."

By the time we got Lia discharged, Asher had filled my house with her clothes, blankets, and cases of fancy vegan baby formula—the only type we could find in Climax without dairy on short notice. I left her to get settled in when Gran called to say she was fixing to puree the entire house. I suspect we will all be on a liquid diet alongside Lia.

I don't exactly own a tea service, so Gran sent me with a kettle and a mesh strainer, with instructions for steeping the basement herbs. I halt in my doorway and nearly drop the basket when I see Lia through the open doorway to my bedroom.

She stands with her back to me, shirtless, the glorious line of her spine on display for an instant as she tugs a sweatshirt over her head. *No bra.*

I chastise myself for thinking these kinds of thoughts about a woman who just got out of the hospital. I clear my throat to announce my presence and she whips around, startled.

"Ethan."

I hold up the basket. "Gran sent stuff to make tea. She's got a vat of soup she's making for tomorrow."

Lia wrings her hands and looks around my cabin. "This is all really too much. I'm practically a stranger."

I set the basket on the counter and fill the kettle from the tap, keeping one eye on my almost forever. "You could never be a stranger here." The gas burner clicks and lights and I go about sliding the strainer into one of my mugs to make Lia's tea. "I forgot to ask if you even want a cup of tea."

She smiles. "Tea would be perfect." Lia walks into the living room and sits hesitantly on the couch, one arm across her middle. "I still don't know where you'll sleep?"

I tip my chin at the couch as the kettle begins to whistle. I pour the hot water into the mug, watching the tiny plants swirl and float inside the strainer. "Hell, I fall asleep on the couch half the time anyway."

Lia snickers. "Colleen said you slept with Baabara a few weeks ago."

I snort a laugh and carry the mug, along with a jar of honey and a spoon, over to the couch. "I did do that, yes. So, you can see, the couch is an upgrade."

Lia reaches for the mug and inhales. "Oh, this smells so nice. Is that fresh chamomile?"

I nod. "I just learned that Gran has an indoor garden operation in the basement. She's got lights and lumens and a humidity monitor."

Lia makes an impressed face. "I should ask what her summer plans are for all of it. Maybe there's something we can add into the grant."

I scratch my head and lean against the wall, not sure if I should sit next to Lia on the sofa, if that would make her uncomfortable. "I know she moves some of it outside, but I doubt she's got anything to the scale we'd need for farm grants."

Lia blows on the tea. "You'd be surprised. People can pack a lot into a small space if they use the land strategically." She sets the mug on the coffee table and claps her hands. "Oh, I wonder if we could couch it as a healing garden! Mint, chamomile…do you know if she's doing echinacea or witch hazel? Shoot, where is my laptop?"

I pull the notebook from my back pocket and thumb past the pages of notes I took regarding Lia's care. "Here. You can write down your questions and ask her in the morning. I'm sure Asher forgot to bring your work stuff."

Lia arches a brow. "What makes you say that?"

I shrug. "Because he's freaking out about his own

work." I decide to just go ahead and sit next to Lia on the couch, watching her sip at her tea and scratch out notes about Gran's garden. "I never wanted that kind of life—stressing about deadlines and spending ten hours sitting in a chair."

"Well, you've got some pretty intense deadlines with the growing cycle. It's just a race against bugs and over-ripening instead of another person tapping a watch."

"I guess that's true."

Lia finishes the tea and sets the mug on the table, sinking into the couch to rest her head on the back. I reach around and grab a Baabara sweater, tucking the huge garment over Lia's lap like a blanket. She smiles and the moment feels so right. Like I've been tucking her in all my life.

"Thank you, Ethan," she whispers, her eyes growing heavy.

"Any time, Lia." I watch as she slowly drifts off beside me, not sure if it's exhaustion or medication taking her under so quickly. I stoop to pick her up, carrying her into my bedroom and setting her into the nest she made of my bed.

By the time I get the kitchen cleaned up and organized, the stress of the day settles in hard. I hadn't realized how afraid I was when Lia was shrieking in pain, hadn't stopped to let myself think about what it meant to see her hurting. I have a long history of stomping down painful memories, telling myself it doesn't do to dwell on those things.

Tonight, it feels important to close my eyes and breathe, to think about how yes, Lia was in agony, but I managed to get her to the hospital. I'm still stunned that the small Climax satellite campus had the sort of doctor Lia needed.

I lie back on the couch, silently expressing my gratitude for that, and then I remember the doctor's larger concerns: that Lia's fancy specialist might have her on the wrong type of medication.

Lia's fancy *boyfriend* specialist.

She has a boyfriend. A boyfriend. If I repeat it to myself enough times, maybe I'll stop thinking about how she looks and smells and makes my stomach flip when she smiles.

I punch at the rock-hard pillow on my couch and roll to my side. It takes me a long time to fall asleep as I worry how I'll ever manage to convince Lia to take a closer look at her health.

# CHAPTER 16
# LIA

I WAKE SLOWLY, CONFUSED. THE SHEETS SMELL UNFAMILIAR, woodsy, and I blink against the sunlight streaming between gaps in heavy, dark curtains. I hear rhythmic metallic clicking nearby and the events of yesterday come flooding back. I'm in Ethan's cabin because of a flare-up.

This condition can be demoralizing...I hate feeling unable to care for myself - the helplessness. And now I'm here with my first boyfriend because I'm too weak to navigate stairs. I'd love to lie here and wallow, but my mouth feels like cotton. I know I need to keep up with my hydration or this will just spiral. Fatigue has already sunk its claws into me, and I'm sluggish as I try to stand up.

Before I get very far, the clicking stops and footsteps approach along the wood plank floor. My chest seizes thinking about Ethan seeing me in his personal space … but then, he must have carried me in here … I fell asleep next to him on the couch.

"Oh good, you're up." His voice comes from the doorway, I turn to meet his gaze, relieved to see the familiar warmth there. No sign of annoyance at having his room co-opted. "How are you feeling today?"

I adjust my weight, my spine twinging a bit. The abdominal pain has dulled, but the pounding in my temples reminds me I need to drink my electrolytes. "Better, I think." I clutch at my throat and clear the scratchiness from my voice. "Still pretty tired."

Ethan nods. "You should take it easy today. I brought you the soup from Gran." He backs into the main room of the cabin, where I see a pot simmering on the stove. The smell is more than I can handle right now, though. I clutch my tummy and slip into the bathroom, feeling grateful that Ethan makes himself busy in the kitchen.

I take care of business and that's when I notice what I assume has been the cause of the sounds this morning. Ethan has installed a fancy bidet attachment to his toilet. Not one of the cheap ones that blast cold water, although that would have been welcome. But this ... this is the deluxe Japanese model, with warm water and pressure settings. It has buttons to change the angle of the spray based on the anatomy of the user.

I coo in relief as I clean up. When I join Ethan in the kitchen, his eyes crinkle at the corners when he smiles. The exhaustion in my bones recedes in the glow of his generosity and thoughtfulness. "Ethan," I rasp, emotion clogging my throat. "Did you build me a bidet?"

He blushes—blushes!—and rubs the back of his neck. "Oh, hey. I wanted to surprise you. I was checking my email like you suggested." He grins and I feel warm all the way down to my toes. "So, then I was looking around online about Crohn's and how nice it is to have a bidet." He shrugs. "I was going to just build something from extra parts, but I ran into Chen in town, and he was about to ship one of these back ... would you believe he bought one for each floor of his house?"

I step closer, reaching for the soft flannel of Ethan's shirt. "I would believe that, yes. Why was he returning one?"

Ethan wraps an arm around me like we've been standing this way for years, like it's normal for us to clutch one another. I almost stretch up to kiss him on the cheek before I remember that I can't do that. He smiles. "Chen's husband said two tush washers is plenty. So, I slipped him some cash and saved him the shipping fee." Tears flood my eyes yet again as I think about the care behind Ethan's gesture. After all these years away, Ethan still wants to make my life better. He is so dedicated to learning what will help. And now I'm standing in my ex-boyfriend's kitchen crying over a butt washer.

"Is it okay? Did I get the right thing?" Worry creeps into his voice at my silence.

I nod and a sob escapes. "No one has ever ..." I swallow around the giant lump of emotion in my throat. "You didn't have to do any of this, Ethan."

He shrugs like it's nothing, because to Ethan, kindness is nothing. He's always taken care of the people around him as best as he could. "I want you to be comfortable, Lia."

And I realize I am. More than I can remember being for a long time. My doctors have always focused on what I need to *give up* to manage my condition ... Ethan thinks about what he can provide.

Overcome with gratitude and feeling seen, I wrap my arms around his waist and press my face into his chest. It feels strange to touch him again after so long, to be this close to him. To smell him. But my god, does it feel good. We stand entwined as my tears soak his shirt and I feel the strong safety as his arms encircle my body.

Eventually, we separate as he clears his throat. "I made you another cup of tea. You seemed to like that last night. And the soup is here keeping warm for you, whenever you're up to it."

I nod and he reaches for his hat. I'm sure he has work to do outside, work he kept waiting while he made me comfortable. "Ethan ... what did you do? After I ended things, I mean ..." Sometimes the ache and shame of cutting him off eats at me more fiercely than my immune system.

Sadness slides across Ethan's face and he clutches the edge of the counter. "Well, I came to look for you, like I said. And I couldn't find you. So, I built a house." He waves an arm around the room. I glance at the cabin with fresh perspective. "Grandad helped me build this place. You know, to take my mind off the sting."

My chest squeezes, faced with the consequences of my choices. "I was so consumed by my illness, Ethan. So mired in doctor's appointments and arguments with insurance. Anything outside of immediate survival was ... out of the question." He swallows and I watch his throat work. "I thought you hated me," I whisper.

Ethan takes my hand, cradling it between both of his. "I've only ever loved you, Lia."

The admission hangs between us, heavy and serious. I'm not sure what to do in the presence of this man and his honesty and the magnitude of his emotions. I lean forward, thinking I might kiss him, knowing that's a mistake.

A bleat from outside interrupts the moment. Mrs. Bedd stomps past the cabin with Baabara on a leash, waving through the front window with a smile on her face.

Ethan pats my hand and heads outside to work. I watch him go and make a silent promise to stop running from him. We can take care of each other now if we let ourselves.

# CHAPTER 17
# LIA

I'M SURPRISED BY HOW COMFORTABLY I FALL INTO A ROUTINE living with Ethan. I feel so at ease in Fork Lick. My energy levels are still quite low, but I'm able to work from bed and, frankly, the Bedd family is meeting all my needs. It's indulgent, decadent. Over the next few days, Ethan's grandmother delivers pureed delicious food every morning with Baabara in tow, sometimes on a leash and sometimes not.

Inevitably, Ethan argues with her about carrying heavy pots all the way from the house and scolds her for not keeping the sheep on a lead.

This morning is no different, and Gran raps on the door bright and early and I see her through the window, wagging a huge jar of mashed sweet potatoes. I hear hooves clacking on the porch and Ethan stalks across the cabin, throwing open the door with a growl. "She's not a dog, Gran. If you want that kind of pet, I can take you to the shelter."

Gran smiles and waves at me and shoves the jar at Ethan. "Speaking of dogs…" She steps into the house and closes the door behind her, leaving the sheep loose outside. I watch from the sofa as Baabara begins to rub herself along Ethan's porch railing before sinking down to nap in the sun.

Ethan strides toward the fridge with the jar. "We weren't speaking of dogs," he mutters.

Gran sinks into one of the chairs at his table and begins straightening the papers piled there. "Your brother Samuel has such a way with dogs…"

Ethan's eyes roll toward the ceiling, I watch him breathe through his nose. Biting back a laugh, I turn to Ethel. "I remember Samuel was always pestering Eugene to get a dog."

She nods. "Well, and now he has his own space and his own hound." She taps on the edge of the table. "I thought we could have him over to look at the strawberries."

Ethan stiffens and grips the edge of the counter. "He has very important work to do." Ethan grunts out the words through gritted teeth. "I'm sure he doesn't have time."

Gran waves a hand. "He'll be here in an hour. I heard on the weather radio that we're expecting storms next week and we want to make sure the seedlings are protected, right?"

Ethan's eyes widen and I watch tension ripple through his body. I lick my lips and suggest, "I'd love to have him look over what I've got so far with the grant application. He's much more familiar with the terminology and we want to make sure we sound like we know what we're talking about when we submit." I feel myself starting to ramble as a muscle ticks in Ethan's neck. Gran beams. "I'm mostly comfortable with the budget and financial statements but I've been sort of winging it with the project narrative."

Gran claps her hands. "There. It's settled. I'm going to make some lunch for you boys. Lia, dear, can you keep an eye on Baabara for me? I think she can tell she's about to see the farrier for a hoof trim and she's been a little extra..."

Before I can protest that I don't know how to look after a sheep, Ethel waves her way out of the cabin with Ethan in hot pursuit. He grumbles and growls about his brother coming to make everything harder than it needs to be.

None of them have mentioned me returning to my brother's house. Asher has barely emerged, texting me briefly that work continues to be intense for him. So ... I just stay here. And pretend this is how my life can be—working from a bright and cozy cabin surrounded by family and the kindest man I ever met.

I glance through my work emails, spying one from my boss demanding an update on the Bedd project. Biting my lip, I fire off a response that I need more time here and that I really think the family has potential to move solidly into the black. I finish my protein shake and hurry outside just as Baabara starts heading toward the strawberry patch. I smile as I see Ethan and Samuel standing side by side. From the back, they look so similar–tall and slim, hips cocked to the right as they stare out at the field. Samuel gestures broadly as Ethan nods. From this vantage point, the conversation seems benign.

I follow Baabara toward the brothers and she halts when Samuel's dog starts yapping at her. Baabara starts jogging toward her enclosure, which I figure is probably a good thing, so I stoop down to pet the dog and listen to Samuel's thoughts on our project.

"You're going to need something to keep the birds off the fruit anyway, Ethan. Even if the hail doesn't get the berries, the crows will."

Ethan puts his hands on his hips and swallows. "How much will this tunnel project cost us? I don't need to tell you funds are tight."

Samuel grins and claps Ethan on the back. "Great news, brother. A few hours of paperwork and this can become a spring break project for crop sciences students."

"Spring break? Damn it, Samuel, I don't want this place to become another Woodstock." I bite back a laugh as Samuel explains how a small group of enthusiastic undergrads can camp in the pole barn for a few days and set up protective mesh tents over each row of the young strawberries as part of an experiential learning program.

A noise from the main house has all of us turning, and Samuel sighs when he sees his dog arguing with Baabara outside her space.

As Samuel jogs off toward the animals, I squeeze Ethan's arm. "Not so bad, right? Having student volunteers here is a good thing for us, Ethan."

He frowns and closes his eyes. "I hate when my brother is right about something."

I laugh at him. "Well, me, too, but you'll get over it eventually." I pinch his cheek and his eyes fly open. "Come on. You can tell your grandmother she gets to cook for a bunch of starving college students."

# CHAPTER 18
# ETHAN

DARK CLOUDS ROLL IN AS I SECURE THE LAST TENTING FRAME over the wimpy little strawberry plants. Eventually I'll admit that Samuel was right about all of this, and that it wasn't too bad having a trio of enthusiastic young people here all week. Today I just want to cover everything before the storm takes out everything we've done so far.

The strawberry cuttings took root surprisingly well considering we're such amateurs. Not even Samuel had anything to say about the quality of our work so far. I hate how disorienting it feels working with something new like this. And why the hell are we going with such a fragile crop anyway? A nice, sturdy soybean crop goes in the ground later and I don't have to worry about this kind of shit. I kick an intact Baabara turd and laugh at the absurdity of it all. Strawberries.

It feels good to have something to occupy my hands right now, though. My brain is a mess, a roller coaster.

Having Lia in my house has been testing every ounce of my emotional strength. I smell her everywhere, think about her all the time. All I want to do is haul her into my arms and kiss the hell out of her, but not only is she in pain, she's dating someone else. Her nearness sets my nerves thrumming. I'm equal parts afraid something terrible will happen to her, turned on, and overcome by lust.

So, I bury myself in my work and do what I can to keep her comfortable. When I installed that water sprayer, I had no idea she'd respond like that ... like I was a hero or something. I'm no hero. I'm barely pulling back the lust monster raging inside me at all times. She seems much better than when she left the hospital, but I'm in no hurry to send her back to Asher's place. Hard as it might be, I prefer having her where I can see that she's healing. Where I can make sure she's safe.

Today, I had the overwhelming urge to kiss her, but I don't want to push her like that. She's a guest in my home, beholden to me right now. I already don't like it that she's dating her doctor ... I don't want to be another man who takes advantage of her when she's trying to get back on her feet. Literally.

I wipe sweat from my brow despite the cool temperature. I heave a sigh and look at the sky again. I don't feel like working in the rain, so it seems I'm about done for the day. I head over to the big house to check in on my grandmother and Baabara before the storms come. Gran greets me on the porch with two mugs of hot tea.

"Thought you might like to sit and sip a bit." She passes a mug to me, eyeing my weariness with concern crinkling her eyes.

We stare out at the rows of green tunnels covering the crops we've hung our hopes on. "You gonna miss having extra people around now that Samuel's students are gone?"

Gran smiles and pats my hand. "It warms these old bones seeing Lia here." Gran blows gently on her steaming tea. "Even if she'd probably prefer my company up at the big house."

I wave a hand at my grandmother. "I told you, Gran. She can't do the stairs. You should see how weak she is. Huge, dark circles under her eyes." I take a sip of the tea. "She says thank you for the sorbet, by the way."

Gran smiles and sinks into a rocker. She's wrapped in a huge wool shawl and between that and the tea, I'm confident she's warm enough to sit outside with me for a little while. The smell of petrichor overpowers the fragrant tea.

"I still can't believe you grow this stuff yourself."

Gran rocks in her chair and we watch the sky. "Your grandfather wasn't a big fan of my gardening…I think he thought it meant he didn't provide enough. Well anyway, it's been keeping me busy since he's been gone." I feel the loneliness in her words. I'm not sure what to say to her, so I just sit with her and think about how I'm no stranger to loss myself.

"Have you been hanging out with your knitting ladies? They seem to have a lot to say."

Gran shakes her head and rocks, "We're on a bit of a hiatus until the weather is more predictable. Nobody likes to drive in a hailstorm."

I place a hand on her knee. "I'd take you where you need to go. You know that."

She smiles and nods. Thunder rattles the windowpanes as we sip and sit. Gran mutters something about her knitting group having to meet over video, I'm glad neither of us has to navigate through a deluge. The first fat raindrops splatter down, signaling my cue to get on home before I get there drenched. I sigh, my muscles protesting as I stand. Gran squeezes my forearm in wordless encouragement. "You and Lia going to make it up to the house for supper tonight?"

I shake my head, both in answer to her question and at the sight of Colleen barreling down the lane, trying to get to the house before the rains come. I kiss Gran on the cheek and give my sister a wave, jogging through the icy drops on the way to my cabin. Baabara bleats at me from inside her house. I fed her plenty of her fancy hay earlier and she has water in there. I'm not concerned about her right now.

My thoughts are with the woman hunkered down in my house, hopefully cozy by the fireplace. I run up the steps and see her through the window. My breath catches at the sight of her there, drowsy eyed, hair mussed, book on her lap. It takes some degree of trust to relax like that in someone else's home. I like that Lia feels that trust. I like it too much.

She looks up and smiles when I enter the room. "I put the soup on in case you were hungry. I saw you had bread … must be nice."

I chuckle as I pull off my boots and hang my jacket on the peg above the rubber tray I bought to protect the floor from drips. "I'm sure we can find you a decent gluten free bread somewhere around here."

She laughs. "Yeah. Maybe over in Coxsackie."

By the time I hurry through a shower, Lia has relocated to the bed. She's got the door shut but I'm extra careful to be quiet as I inhale the bread and soup. It's been a long, hard day of work and avoiding big feelings, so it doesn't take me long to settle into sleep on my couch.

The storm wakes me. A deafening crack of thunder shakes the walls. Lia must have been torn from her own sleep because she appears in the living room, panic etched on her face. I hurry to her side.

"Just noise. You're alright." I smooth the blanket she has draped around her shoulders, wishing I could steady her frayed nerves so easily. She clutches my hand as more thunder booms.

"I forgot where I was again."

I chuckle in the darkness. "Right here at my Bedd Bidet and Breakfast."

Lia groans. "Oh my god, did you work on that all day?"

"Been saving it for the right time." I squeeze her hand and use my other hand to rub her blanketed shoulder. "I promise, you're safe and dry, Lia. Why don't you head back to bed?"

The rain is coming down in torrents and it sounds like maybe some hail along with it.

"Will you..." Lia bites her lip, hesitant vulnerability in her eyes. "Will you lie with me awhile? The thunder is worse in the bedroom."

I nod, pulse racing as she leads me into my own room, she crawls in bed. I lie on top of the blankets beside her, feeling the warmth of her body despite the layers of cotton between us. Another crack of thunder comes with blinding lightning and Lia shudders.

I gather her close, tucking her head beneath my chin and wrapping my arms around her slender frame. Slowly the tremors subside as her muscles uncoil against me. Her voice is a whisper as she says, "the thunder sounds so much like the MRI tubes. I woke up and for a minute I thought I was back in the hospital, in the dark, confined by wires…"

"You're here with me, Lia. And if you have to go to the hospital again, I'll make sure you're not alone. Ever." She exhales a jagged breath and I squeeze her gently. Damp tendrils of her hair cling to my jaw, releasing her sweet floral scent. Without thought I press my lips to the top of her head, eliciting a tiny gasp.

We freeze. I was reckless and forward and I took advantage of her in her fear. Heat creeps up my neck until Lia inches back just far enough to meet my gaze, our eyes having grown accustomed to the dark by now. She presses soft lips to mine, and I release a moan, deepening the kiss. She tastes both familiar and new, and so, so right in my arms.

I don't know how long we kiss—just kiss—but finally the thunder subsides, and she pulls back. "Thank you, Ethan, for making me feel safe."

"Always, Lia." I drop one final kiss to her forehead and stay by her side as she drifts away to sleep.

# CHAPTER 19
# ETHAN

THE STORM PASSES OVERNIGHT BUT MY RESTLESS ANTICIPATION lingers. I don't know what it means that I fell asleep holding Lia, but I know I had no business kissing her. I rise early, not sure what to do about the woman in my bed as I get ready for the day's work.

The rich scent of dark coffee fills the dim kitchen as the coffee maker gurgles to life. I pour a steaming mug, gulping its bitterness to shock some alertness into my foggy brain.

My eyes drift closed savoring the hot liquid before a bleating cry has them flying open.

I dart onto the porch, scanning for the source of distress until I spot a wooly form munching her way toward my house, her snout nudging away the plastic tenting I installed yesterday to protect the strawberry seedlings.

"Baabara!" I shout, nearly upending my mug as I sprint toward her. She looks up, tender green stems dangling from the side of her mouth. How did the blasted ewe get loose? She acts like she didn't see me and keeps on chewing the tiny leaves meant to save all our butts.

I lunge to grab her but she dances away, trotting farther down the planting row and leaving trampled seedlings in her wake. Baabara stops periodically to sample more foliage as I chase her, hollering in my bare feet. My pulse pounds at the damage she could wreak on our first fledgling crops.

Exasperated, I toss my empty mug aside, hearing it crack against the tenting frame amidst Baabara's indignant bleating as I finally get hold of her collar. She kicks her back hooves, displeased at the interruption of her meal. I wrestle the cursed sheep toward her home, rage simmering in my gut. This feels like divine retribution for me putting my mouth where I shouldn't. I hate that my weakness could destroy everything my family holds dear.

Several rows are clearly ruined, tender plants uprooted by Baabara's assault. Hundreds of dollars and weeks of nurturing in the pole barn destroyed as soon as we got the plants in the damn ground. I shove Baabara into her enclosure, securing the gate.

Surveying the ravaged crop, grief and stress boil over at how one simple misstep might doom everything. I roar in frustration, gripping my hair as unfamiliar tears blur my vision.

Gentle hands cover mine, easing them down. I blink rapidly to clear my eyes and find Lia studying me in the cold. Wordlessly she pulls my trembling body against hers, saying nothing as I inhale ragged breaths, seeking composure.

In this moment, I'm feeling all my losses. My blood boils for my lost parents, my grandfather, his betrayal, and now the loss of the potential solution I worked so hard to first accept and then set into motion.

Lia just stands there holding me while I count my breaths, trying not to strangle the sheep.

Eventually I straighten, scrubbing both hands down my face before witnessing the damage over Lia's shoulder. She follows my gaze, exhaling softly. "We can likely still get a decent harvest. And honestly, Ethan, I think the rain did as much damage as Baabara." Her voice sounds steady despite the fearful shine in her eyes.

I know Lia needs tangible success here as much as anyone. The farm's fate and her career credibility are tied together, and she needs results to convince the bank not to foreclose on our loans. I doubt her bosses want to hear about pampered livestock on a bender. Lia convinced me to try this experiment despite my stubborn resistance and now we both feel the increased fragility of our future.

"Give me a damage estimate for the grant paperwork." Lia tries to keep her tone business-like but I hear the tension at the edge. She moves slowly toward my house, pausing as if she's dizzy. I lag behind, still feeling sour and wondering how in the hell Baabara got out of her bungalow to start with.

When I get back to the cabin and clean off my feet, Lia sits silently at the table staring fixedly at piles of paperwork. Gran always said still waters run deep, and I sense Lia's fears churning beneath her calm.

I remember what happened last night—how I kissed her and she kissed me back. I swallow a lump and long to run across the room and just haul her into my bed, farm and finances be damned.

Before I can ruminate too long, Lia looks up. Her face is still clearly carrying her fatigue. "We will get through this, Ethan," she vows. "I believe that now."

She said "we."

I open my mouth to ask her if she meant to say "we," but my door bursts open and Gran stomps into my house. "Did you see what my beautiful Baabara did to our plants? Oh, Ethan! How did she get so naughty?"

Colleen is close on Gran's heels, scowling. "Maybe it's because you spoil her, Gran. You could try spoiling one of us instead and send the sheep to the barn like a regular farm animal..."

Gran clutches her chest. "Baabara is not regular, Colleen Murphy Bedd. You bite your tongue. I never see you complaining about your merino wool socks and sweaters that sheep provides."

Lia laughs. "I can't tell—are we angry with Baabara or grateful for her services to the fiber community?"

Gran harrumphs. "How bad is it, Ethan? The damage?"

I sink into the chair opposite Lia, still barefoot, still wishing I had coffee. "Hard to say. I never grew strawberries before, so I don't know how much I should expect to lose."

Colleen peers outside. "It looks like you covered almost everything with hoops and tents? So at least the hail didn't get it?"

I nod and sigh.

Colleen taps her foot and looks at me. "You know who knows these kinds of things?"

I hold up a hand. "Don't say it. Come on."

She shakes her head. "Our brothers are freaking farm geniuses. Alex is a 15-minute drive down the road and you can't get over yourself and go ask him for manure. Sam's got a master's degree in Soil and Crop Science from an Ivy League University but neither you nor Gramps ever take his ideas seriously." She steps closer to me with each word and starts poking me in the chest with her surprisingly pointy index finger.

I hold my hand up. "I already took in Sam's damn students, Colleen. What more do you want from me?"

She flings her hands in the air. "Call Alex. Make up. Stop being a butthead."

With a final eye roll, Colleen swirls out of my house. Gran winces and waves and follows her, calling after Baabara in a voice most people reserve for tiny babies.

Lia bites her lip and I can tell she's trying not to laugh. "Did your sister call you a butthead?"

I squint at her. "Like your brother never calls you names."

# CHAPTER 20
# LIA

ONCE ETHAN COOLS DOWN, I REMIND HIM THAT HE'S GOING to need to hire help for the pick-your-own adventures. Much as I'd cherish the opportunity to be fully hands-on with the project I'm spearheading, I know my physical limitations. I'd spend more time in the rented port-o-potties than in the pole barn if they put me in charge of concessions.

Ethan heads outside with a wave and soon I hear him discussing the staffing with Mrs. Bedd, who has Baabara on a leash out for a walk—perhaps to survey her handiwork. I watch through the window as Ethel starts gesturing wildly.

"I know someone! I know someone who would be perfect. I found her on the internet."

Ethan's brows shoot up so high they disappear under his ski cap. "You found a woman online?"

Mrs. Bedd waves a hand. "There's a website for those people who live in vans. They convert them into tiny houses and just drive around doing odd jobs. I was looking at renting out the field behind the pole barn."

I step closer to the window, eager to hear more about this scheme and worried about how it fits into our carefully mapped out plans to meet the grant application requirements. The pole barn is mostly an empty space for storage and equipment, but there's a small office that Ethan never uses, and a full bathroom next to it. Ethel continues to explain that there's a service where farms with extra land can rent it out to people needing work. "Everyone wins!" I'm instantly skeptical about an online connection, but I can also tell the idea of interviewing and hiring someone is far outside Ethan's comfort zone.

I think back to our kiss last night, something I never should have let happen, and I decide Ethan has strayed far enough from his comfort zone on my account.

But Ethel continues, saying, "I found a gal the other day. Ethan, you finish up here and then you can do one of those Zoomy thingies. You can tell her what we need specifically."

Ethan flushes. "Hell, Gran, I don't even know what we need."

Gran waves a hand; Baabara bleats. "Bring Lia with you. She knows."

Having delivered marching orders, Ethel struts back toward the house, sparing me a wave where I'm spying from Ethan's window. I suppose that's today sorted.

In the meantime, I soak my aching joints in Ethan's deep tub until my hands prune, the hot water loosening tight muscles made worse lately by tension and activity exacerbating my illness.

Lying back cloaked in lavender-scented steam, I finally relax fully for the first time in ages, my thoughts drifting to Ethan. To kissing Ethan. To how good it felt, especially compared with my recent feelings toward Richard.

My thoughts circle back to Richard assuring me he talked to his medical advisors about our relationship, but he's also apparently treating me off the books. Everything about him sets me on edge lately, and then Ethan holds me when I'm scared and quietly builds me a bidet without being asked. I let myself relax in the deliciously hot water, trying to make sense of all my confusing feelings.

# CHAPTER 21
# LIA

I JOLT HEARING THE SCREEN DOOR SLAP SHUT LATER, realizing I dozed off. The bathwater is chilly, along with my body. Wincing, I rise slowly, wrapping myself in Ethan's robe that engulfs my frame. I'm thankful he didn't walk in on me naked and exposed in his bathroom. But then I wonder if that would really be so bad...

Ethan calls my name just as I secure the robe's belt. I emerge from the bathroom, combing dripping hair from my eyes. Concern creases his face. "Everything okay?"

I wave dismissively. "Just tired. Did I miss your zoom?" My casual words sound strained even to me. Ethan regards me silently as he removes his hat and coat.

"You're sure you're alright?"

My defenses sharpen in answer to his probing tone. "Yes, fine. Tell me about this *gal* your grandmother found." I aim for nonchalance again but internally cringe hearing the turn in my voice. I can't just be cool around Ethan, at least not until I figure things out with Richard.

Ethan's eyes narrow, seeing through my front. He

crosses the room and grips my shoulders. "First, you're going to eat something. You're dead on your feet."

He busies himself heating another puree Gran sent while I pick at a jar of apricot baby food, my stomach unsettled.

"So, this person seems capable?" I force out. Ethan nods and describes her Jill-of-all-trades background as he sits across from me. I try focusing on his words and not my churning insides.

"She needs a place to park her van. She'll be living onsite, so having her handle festival prep should be easy."

The Bedd family is making a habit of taking in women with nowhere else to go. I stab my spoon harder than necessary. "And your Gran found her online?"

"On some site for transient workers looking for temporary housing." Ethan gulps his soup. "She actually seems like a godsend. As we were talking, she whipped up a logo and website to market the thing. We just need to nail down locations for parking fields, port-a-potties...."

His words fade to background noise as I imagine a hippie waif just perfect for Ethan, invading the farm I helped revive. Gran said Ethan needs her. Gran, lonely and grieving, wants her close by. Ethan *should* be pining after this sort of woman. I'm taken, even if I did kiss another man in a moment of weakness when I was scared.

I have a freaking boyfriend. Don't I? I feel like the worst woman in the world. I already broke Ethan's heart once. What am I doing here in Fork Lick, in his house? Bile rises in my throat, I push away the barely touched food.

"Whoa, take it slowly if you aren't hungry." Ethan presses the back of his hand to my clammy forehead. "No fever at least. Go lie down. I'll clean up."

I let him guide me to the sofa, hating my weakness. My illness always emerges at the worst times — when I need fortitude to power through professional challenges or navigate emotional pits like jealous fits over virtual strangers. Pathetic.

I must doze again, waking disoriented by a quilt tucked around me. The room darkens into dusk. Hearing Ethan shuffling paper at the table, I rise gingerly, combing tangled hair with my fingers.

"Morning, sunshine." Ethan doesn't look up from leafing through folders...likely paperwork for hiring Molly, the cute pixie van woman who's sure to capture his heart. If only I wasn't having a flare up, then maybe I could be more helpful, and they wouldn't have to hire anyone. My stomach knots anew.

"Very funny. What time is it anyway?"

"Nearly six. You think the grant committee will go for all of this? I feel like all I did was spread some poop and drive a tractor ...."

I nod mutely, arms crossed. Ethan caps his pen, studying me. "Lia, are we alright?"

"Of course. Why wouldn't we be?" Too bright and too fast. Ethan stands, slowly approaching me. I fight not to step back, hating that he witnesses my unease.

"Hey..." Strong hands grip my shoulders as his blue-eyed gaze bores into mine. "Talk to me."

My composure cracks. "I shouldn't have kissed you. It's not fair. And then, once you get Molly settled, I will probably go because...I'd be done." Hot tears threaten as I voice a fear I didn't realize I had — being unnecessary and replaceable. If I'm done here, that means I head back to the city and ... I don't know if I want that. Not anymore.

Ethan sweeps me against his chest, lips pressing my hair. "Don't ever think that, Lia. You're saving this place when no one else could. You're fighting for our farm."

I want him to say he'll fight for *us*. But I have no right to hope for another chance with him. Although ... as he holds me, wearing his robe, standing in his house where he kissed me ... maybe it's not a foregone conclusion that he'll never give me another chance.

I cling to him, the knot inside loosening. We stand entwined as a lump rises in my throat. "I need to call my doctor," I whisper. "Update him."

Ethan tenses. "Your *boyfriend?* You sure that's wise?"

I extricate myself, bristling at his judgmental tone. I forgot his unpleasant opinion of my doctor-boyfriend after recent arguments over my care. In fact, I forgot that I have a boyfriend. "I just want his medical opinion."

Ethan snorts. "Yeah, 'cause that's worked great so far."

Anger flares now, and I know it's not fair to Ethan. "You still don't know everything!" I burst out. "Stop acting like you grasp complex immunology!"

Hurt flashes across Ethan's face. Shit. I press my palms over my eyelids as shame replaces fury. "I'm sorry...I didn't mean..."

Ethan turns away, muscles coiled. "It's fine. You should call your boyfriend. I'm sure he's been missing you." He snatches his coat off its hook. The door slams loudly behind him. I flinch, hot tears spilling down my cheeks. Why do I keep lashing out at the one person wholly on my side? What kind of person am I, letting Ethan kiss me—

kissing him back—when I've got a boyfriend? A boyfriend I rarely see and who hasn't checked in on me once since this flare…

I have no idea what's going on in my head. In one breath I'm heartbroken at the idea of leaving this place once my job here is done. The next, I'm dreading any contact with my life back in the city. Especially with Richard. I wait several minutes for my breath to steady before fixing a smile I don't feel and clicking on Richard's contact for a video call. Right away his distracted tone clues me in that he's working. "Lia. How are things?"

I tell him about the sheep eating the seedlings, but he doesn't seem to notice. His "mm hmm" feels robotic and he barely looks up from his paperwork as I talk. I sigh, and pivot to his area of interest: Crohn's disease.

I summarize my symptoms and medication adjustments, asking his opinion on lowering my riskier oral medications. Richard makes noncommittal sounds, only half listening. "Babe, you know tapering those caused complications before. And it's unethical for me to directly advise without seeing you."

I press my case, but Richard cuts me off. "Sorry to do this, babe. I've actually got a consult. Just stay the course and we'll discuss next steps when you're back in the city."

He ends the call abruptly. My pulse quickens, reading the subtext. Richard is not interested in making time for me, either as a patient or a partner. I squeeze my burning eyes shut. All the old feelings of being managed versus supported creep back in. What in the hell am I doing with Richard?

I log in to my online health portal, looking at my most recent labs. Asher used to obsess over my results, back when nobody would listen to me that something was wrong. He used to make charts and bar graphs for me. It's been a long time since I looked at my own numbers. I'd been trusting all my care to Richard.

I check my numbers and am shocked to see wildly irregular inflammation and nutritional markers. I look up interactions between my infusions and various oral meds. The data makes Dr. Sanchez's conservative suggestions seem wise, not detrimental as Richard insisted.

It's nearly dark by the time I hear footsteps outside again. I steel myself to face Ethan's skepticism, but his expression shows only bone-deep weariness when he appears.

"No holes in Baabara's bungalow. She must've slipped under the gate itself." He braces thick arms on the table. "Maybe electric fencing is the solution. Those can run a couple grand though, even DIY-ing parts. Plus, Gran would worry Babs would shock herself." He scrubs both hands down his face. "I'm open to suggestions if you think of any."

There's defeat in his voice now instead of accusation. He looks utterly exhausted, the battered commander of a struggling platoon. My cheeks burn in the silence.

"Ethan, about before...."

He waves off my apology. "It doesn't matter. You're worn out and lashing out happens."

"It does matter." I grasp his calloused hand firmly. "I deeply regret questioning your intelligence or your judgment. You're the most capable person I know."

Ethan blinks rapidly at my vehement tone. Slowly he brings our joined hands to his lips and brushes a whisper-soft kiss over my knuckles. "Well Ms. Thorne, I happen to think you're alright too." The tender moment stretches until Ethan clears his throat gruffly. "You talk to your doctor then?"

I frown. "Briefly. He insists the oral meds stay for now despite side effects. But after we spoke, I dug into my latest test results..." I detail my discoveries around nutritional imbalances and biochemical markers potentially indicating toxicity.

Ethan listens intently, asking a few questions. The more I talk, the more it becomes clear that there is nothing to consider with Richard. I no longer trust him as a physician or a romantic partner. "I ... think I want to try to visit Dr. Sanchez again over in Climax. I'm thinking she might be onto something about stopping the harsh oral meds," I conclude. "The infusions might control symptoms well enough alone."

Ethan considers for a long moment, thumb grazing his bottom lip. "And this goes against your boyfriend's medical advice?" I bristle briefly at his phrasing but merely nod. "Okay then. When do we call up Dr. Sanchez?"

There's no judgment or skepticism now. Just solid support bolstering my conviction. I exhale fully for the first time all day.

# CHAPTER 22
# LIA

I STARE AT MY REFLECTION IN DREARY DAWN LIGHT, NOTING the pallor of my skin, dark circles framing my eyes. I'm more fatigued than ever despite spending more than twelve hours in Ethan's bed. I could feel the aura of his concern for me from the living room. I hate how my feelings about him are entwined with my growing discomfort with my *boyfriend*.

The more time I spend apart from Richard, the more I see that he really doesn't do anything to earn that title. I know I have to make a change, but much like the Bedd family, I'm terrified in the face of doing so. My hands shake slightly, like my body and brain are equally exhausted, as I try applying mascara. The wand clatters into the sink. I abandon the effort with a defeated sigh.

"This stops today. No more letting him control you." My whispered promise echoes in the small bathroom. I've sacrificed autonomy over my care, my living situation, even my diet to accommodate Richard's directives for far too long. The blind trust once so reassuring now feels like willful ignorance, my health held hostage to convenience

Richard's ambitions over serving my quality of life. Things can be different. Things already are different.

Resolution solidifying, I shuffle to the kitchen, finding Asher in Ethan's house. I'm grateful he responded to my cryptic text message, even if he's going to be obnoxious about helping me. My brother smirks at me. "You dragged me out of bed before nine a.m. for an urgent meeting and you're just getting up?"

I pour myself a cup of tea and give him the finger, then steel my nerves to reveal my plans. "How long have I got you?"

He swallows a mouthful of coffee. "I can spare a few hours. Already dropped off more baby food for you. Ethan's out digging holes or whatever farmers do."

I arch a brow and shake my head and set my tea on the counter. "I wondered if you could take me to visit Dr. Sanchez again in Climax."

Asher's eyes go wide. He grips the counter edge, eyes revealing his surprise that I'm clearly doing something outside Richard's advice. I already know Asher hates that I'm dating Richard and thinks my doctor is a snake. I no longer feel like contradicting him on this point. I swallow. "I've been looking at my numbers. Isn't it you who always says data doesn't have emotions? Only answers?"

Asher grins and dangles his car keys in the air. "That's a bit of a paraphrase. But I'm happy to haul you to Climax. This sounds promising, kid."

"Can you not call me that?" I shoulder him playfully as I reach for my coat and happily climb into my brother's car as we head into town to talk protocol with a doctor who doesn't seem to think of herself as a celebrity. I squeeze Asher's forearm before entering the hospital.

"Whatever happens, I know you've always had my back."
He shuts his eyes against a wave of emotion.

After Asher leaves, I bury myself in non-Bedd work and am pleasantly surprised by how quickly I can get everything done. Without the distractions of the office – or the anxiety that I'll have a bathroom emergency there – I'm so much more efficient. My manager even praises the fast turnaround for a few of the spreadsheets we thought would take me another few days.

High on the success, I decide to do something nice for Ethan, to make up for snapping at him but also because I want to be able to do nice things for people sometimes. Given my current circumstances, the best I can muster is warming up some lunch for us from the leftovers crowding Ethan's fridge. At least I know the man is always appreciative of food.

I locate some rice and decide to combine a few of the soups, tying it all together with some of the herbs Ethel left in a sweet little jar on Ethan's counter. He walks in the front door, sniffing, just as I'm snapping off the burner to ladle the soup into bowls. "Hey," I greet him. "Have lunch with me?"

"Sounds fantastic. Smells delicious." Ethan grins and hurries to the sink to wash his hands. I try not to stare at his methodical process, at the strong fingers scrubbing at his palms. I busy myself setting the table and swoon a little bit when he sits across from me, a smile splitting his face. He takes a huge bite of the soup and his brows shoot up. "Did you make something new? This is great."

I swallow my own bite, feeling proud. "I just blended some things together." He nods and eats hungrily. I wait a few bites before I say, "I have an appointment. With Dr. Sanchez."

Ethan nods. "Good." He reaches across the table and squeezes my hand. "I'm glad you're getting another opinion, Lia. Your health is important."

I smooth my hair back behind my ears and nod. "I know I told you things are complicated with Richard." I close my eyes and take a deep breath. "I actually think it's not complicated. I don't want him, Ethan. Not at all."

Ethan clenches his jaw and I see the muscles of his face and neck working as he decides what to say. His gaze bores into me and he finally says, "You always have a home here, Lia. And I will always do anything I can to help you feel safe and healthy."

I nod rapidly and take another bite of soup while I will myself not to cry. "I know that, Ethan. I forgot for awhile, but I know it now." I glance out the window at the farm, at the trees surrounding my brother's house beyond. "It's good for me, being back here. In so many ways."

Ethan smiles. "Stay as long as you want, then. It's good for me to have you here." His cheeks turn pink, like he admitted something scandalous, and I chuckle.

We finish our soup as I tell him about the charts Asher put together, and I circle my appointment with Dr. Sanchez on the calendar, comforted to know my stay here doesn't have an expiration date.

# CHAPTER 23
# LIA

DR. SANCHEZ FROWNS AT HER COMPUTER SCREEN AS I SIT uncomfortably in the chair across from her. She scours my medical records, looks at charts Asher whipped up based on the results and symptom logs. For years, I've been combining the infusions with oral medications typically prescribed for cancer patients. The side effects have been intense, but I've been so functional … compared to when I could barely scrape myself off the floor.

I see now, as I explain the reality of my daily life to Dr. Sanchez, that my "stable" is still quite impaired. And I can tell from her face that she believes things can be better. "I really want you to wean off the oral meds, Lia. Have you looked over some of the more recent studies?"

I shake my head, because Richard claimed he was helping to produce those studies—he kept telling me I was part of his "cutting-edge research." My pulse quickens and Asher grunts from his chair beside me, his arms crossed over his chest, posture rigid and radiating anger.

I've been bending my life around this illness for years. I

close my eyes against a tear at the thought of what I've given up in the name of self-preservation.

Dr. Sanchez smiles and folds her hands on her desk. "Look, I know I'm just a simple doc in a bumpkin hospital." She rolls her eyes at the stereotype. "But my fellow GI specialists have seen great outcomes from gentler treatment protocols. I truly believe we can keep your symptoms managed and give you more energy, fewer flare-ups, and a life less focused on toilets."

I bark out a laugh, surprised at her candor, but I quickly begin trembling, overwhelmed at her affirmation of my secret fears. Dr. Sanchez is offering to slice a tether and give me something I've never, ever felt I had, options. I press my palms over my eyes and take a few breaths.

"Lia, what are you thinking? Talk to me." Dr. Sanchez's voice is soothing and calm. I hear her insisting that I'm a partner in this discussion. This feels so different from when I was 20 years old, begging for someone to listen to me, and then blindly accepting their advice the second they agreed my symptoms weren't all in my head.

I clear my throat and look over to my brother, whose eyes meet mine in silent encouragement. "I, um, I want change. Can you tell me what you think things would look like? Ongoing?"

Dr. Sanchez shrugs. "Definitely continue the low FODMAP diet, since that's working really well for you. Have you introduced solids again since I saw you last? You're looking much better, by the way."

I shake my head. "Still doing the pureed soups and protein shakes."

"Baby formula," Asher grunts again, shaking his head. "She's drinking baby formula."

"It's for adults, too," I snap at him. Feeling infantilized is a huge part of my hang-up with my entire situation. "But I'm sick of it. I'm sick of outlandish rents in the city just so I can be close to a major research hospital at all times. I hardly ever fly down to see my parents in Florida … and this is my first time back in Fork Lick to see my brother. God, I don't want to live this way anymore."

I realize the truth of it all, that I hate going into an office full-time only to be chained to the office toilet. I hate never taking vacations. I hate not having a community outside the nurses in my doctor's office. Since I've been here, since I begged to come here and help save the Bedd family from ruin, I've felt more whole than I had in decades, despite a flare up that landed me in the hospital.

A few minutes later, Dr. Sanchez has me set up with the admin team for her practice within the hospital at Climax. I don't even have to call Richard's office to transfer my records if I don't want to, although I do want to say goodbye to Javier and Lynn. Best of all, I can do all my bloodwork and infusions right here … a twenty-minute drive from Asher's house…from Ethan.

In the parking lot, I sink into my brother's arms, relief threatening to tip me over. He pats my hair and grips my arms, looking into my eyes. "You never have to see that fucker Richard again."

I laugh at his vehemence. "Maybe one more time," I tell him. "I owe it to Ethan to fully sever those ties."

Asher raises a brow. "Ethan, huh?"

I nod. "Yeah. Ethan."

He smiles briefly and unlocks his car. "I figured." Asher turns on the car and backs out of his parking spot, eyes on the road as he adds, "You should break up with Richard via text. Then block his number."

"Oh, that's your best romantic advice?" I laugh at his matter-of-fact approach, but he's not wrong. A quick text is about as much attention as Richard's given me or my care. For once, I decide to follow my big brother's advice.

I fire off a message:

> It's over. I'm transferring my care to another practice. We're through.

Asher sings along with the radio while he drives, off-tune and missing half the words. I smile and join him, feeling light and happy, eager to get to Ethan. My phone rings and I see that it's Richard calling, but I send the call to voicemail.

He calls again and Asher lowers the volume on the radio. I meet his eyes and answer. "Richard, this isn't a good time for me to talk. I'm very busy."

"Lia, you're being irrational. I'd assume your text was a statement of some kind, but my team tells me they got a records request..."

"Was there information missing from the request? I'm happy to speak with the admin team."

Richard huffs. "Lia, come on. Don't be stupid. You've been gone too long. You need to get back on your meds, get your head on straight."

A wave of calm washes over me as Richard scolds me. I hear him showing me who he really is, and for once I believe him. Richard isn't benevolent and he's not my hero. I don't want anything he has to offer. More importantly, I don't *need* any of it. I've got people on my side now, and they deserve all of my attention. I cut Richard off mid-sentence as he mutters about his research. "What's that? There's such bad reception here in the sticks. My people will be in touch about my medical records. We don't need to speak again."

I hang up the phone and turn the volume back up on the radio. Asher and I sing terribly, and neither of us seems surprised when he skips his driveway and heads directly for Bedd Fellows Farm.

# CHAPTER 24
# ETHAN

I WAS TOO ANXIOUS EVEN TO CHOP WOOD WHILE I WAITED FOR Lia to get back from her appointment with Dr. Sanchez, so I decided it was finally time to take her advice and set up the Wi-Fi in my cabin. She's been doing some work from bed using a hotspot for internet access, and if I'm serious about keeping her here with me, I need to make sure she feels fully welcome. She's been at my place for weeks, but if it were up to me she'd stay forever.

Plus, she keeps insisting I need to check my email.

So … I do. And what I find in there has me holding my breath.

*Dear Mr. Bedd:*

*On behalf of the grant committee from the New York State Department of Agriculture, it is my pleasure to inform you that your business, Bedd Fellows Farm, has successfully obtained our community and sustainable agriculture grant funding.*

I stop reading and jump out of my chair, letting out a loud whoop, and immediately sprint up to the big house. "Gran! Colleen! We got it!"

Gran pokes her head around the corner from her chair

in the living room, where she's got a big pile of knitting on her lap. Colleen, half asleep on the couch reading a book with a naked man on the cover, raises a brow.

"What did you get, dear?" Gran keeps knitting, her needles clacking a steady rhythm along with my heartbeat.

"The grant! We got the MONEY." I scoop Gran out of her seat and spin her around a few times as she protests. I set her down and smack a kiss on her forehead. "Lia did it!"

"What did I do?" Lia's voice comes through the kitchen right behind me and I turn to see her standing there with Asher, both looking pleased.

I point toward the sky, where I can only assume the internet lives. "I got an email. We got the grant, Lia!"

Colleen sits up and gently tucks a bookmark into her novel before setting it on the table. "What's everyone doing here? Can someone elaborate?"

Asher's deep voice booms above everyone's head as he says, "Lia sorted out her meds. She can stay here in Fork Lick if she wants."

"Get out the Old Crow," Gran shouts, clapping her hands. "Call your brothers. I'm happy as a cow in clover, Ethan."

The thought of Grandad's whiskey sours my stomach, but I'm not going to be the one to rain on the celebration. Colleen points at me and says, "I think Ethan should be the one to call Alex and Samuel with this news. Ethan, weren't you calling them for strawberry pointers anyway?"

I scratch at the back of my neck. Between the storm and Lia at my house and cleaning up from Baabara's mini-feast I haven't taken the time to patch things up with my brothers yet. Colleen frowns at me and starts tapping away at her phone. "Fine. I'll text them. But this isn't the end of things, Ethan. You've still got work to do."

"Yes, I know. I know. Ash, will you stay for a drink?" I reach past my grandmother, who is stretching to pull down glasses for all of us. She hasn't yet commented on the depleted stash of whiskey in the once-full bottle.

"Thank you, Ethan, dear. Oh, someone needs to tell Molly she's got a job. She's gotta drive here from…West Virginia I think."

Asher wrinkles his nose. "Who is Molly?"

Lia eyes me intently as I explain that she's a part-time hire to help set up and run sales during the strawberry harvest. "She's got retail experience. And she's good with people," I add, which has Asher nodding in understanding. He and I both hate crowds and all the noise that comes with them. "That reminds me, Ash, we're going to have a lot of people coming in and out of the property in about a month. Sorry for all the extra traffic that will bring."

He waves a hand. "I've got my office insulated. And you know I have security cameras." He accepts the glass of whiskey from Gran and sniffs it, recoiling at the smell of the strong, cheap alcohol. I dash outside and back to my house to grab my phone and send Molly a message. Colleen had to teach both me *and* Gran how to use this new-fangled app for vanlifers, which I didn't even know was a word, nevermind something people did.

I trot back to the house, sparing a moment to flip Baabara the bird as she munches hay in her front yard. Alex arrives as I reach the porch steps and I wait for him to get out of the truck with his dog.

"Hey." He tips a chin at me.

"Hey." I sigh. "Maybe I can buy you dinner someday soon. Talk to you about some things?"

He shrugs. "I hear there's some good news. I can always eat."

We walk into the kitchen to find Asher drumming his hands on the table as Colleen balances a spoon on the tip of her nose. Gran applauds the ridiculous stunt and Alex slides into the seat beside her, plucking the spoon from her face as everyone else groans.

"Sam can't get away in the middle of the day, he says to tell you. Should we get this show on the road?"

Gran takes her place by the stove and looks around her kitchen, overflowing with noise and loved ones. She places a hand on her chest. "It's no secret things have been hard around here." She wipes at a tear in her eye. "I had no idea Eugene was leaving things in such disarray ... but I'm grateful you've all played a part in helping turn this drought into a harvest." Gran lifts her glass of whiskey, we all follow suit. "To the Bedd Fellows Farm family," she says, and we all echo those words before slamming back our drinks.

The room erupts in coughs and sputters as the burning liquid scalds throats all around. I glance at Lia, who hasn't drunk hers. If she can't even handle raw vegetables right now, there's no way this whiskey will feel good in her belly. I shake my head as she stares at the glass and she nods, setting her still-full cup on the counter.

A few minutes later, we manage to sneak away as Asher starts arguing with Gran about something called TikTok and Alex scowls at both of them.

Back at my cabin, I long to ask Lia what Asher meant

about her being able to stay in Fork Lick. I long to know what the doctor said. Most of all, I want to know if she's still spoken for or if it's okay for me to respond to the lust threatening to tear me in half. "You had a big day, it sounds like."

She nods, licking her lip nervously. I stare at her tongue as it sweeps across the seam of her mouth. "So much is going to change, Ethan." I clench at her words, willing myself to be patient as she gathers her thoughts. "I cut ties with Richard. Medically and otherwise."

My eyes must convey the barely contained lust inside me at the thought of Lia being free, Lia being fair game for me to woo. I take a step toward her and let my fingers trail across her jaw, smooth bath her hair, and stare into her dark eyes. "Oh yeah?"

She nods. "And I'm changing my meds. It might be a rocky process for a few weeks … but then I should be able to do so much more."

"Like what?" I step closer still, letting a hand cradle her hip, feeling the small movements in her body as she inhales and exhales.

Lia swallows and I watch her throat. I could watch her endlessly. "Like, stay awake for 12 hours at a time." Lia giggles and rests a hand on my chest.

Breathing through my nose, I catch her scent. It fills my house like it belongs here, like Lia is permeating the atmosphere where I live. "What do you want to do with all that awake time?" I need her to be clear with me. I need Lia to make the next move.

She doesn't answer me with words, stretching up on her toes instead to plant a kiss on my cheek, just past the corner of my lip. With that invitation, I dive into her mouth with mine, thrusting my tongue between her lips, tracing her teeth, moaning at the pleasure of feeling her pressed against me.

Her breasts are small and firm against my stomach, her hands clutching at my flannel shirt as she tries to pull me closer, closer. Still holding her by the hip, I pull her against my hardness, letting her feel how much I want her. She gasps, breaking our kiss to look into my eyes.

"Ethan." Her word is a request and a demand. I tug her against me, both arms on her hips, rubbing her against me until I'm greedy and desperate. Lia shoves me backwards and we frog march toward my bedroom, lips busy sipping each other's skin.

I've been missing this woman for over ten years, and when she finally shoves me back against the mattress, I'm falling physically and emotionally, right over the edge and into the soft bedding as she straddles my hips. "Ethan, I want you so much."

"I—you—gorgeous."

Lia whips her shirt off her head, revealing the soft curve of her belly and creamy breasts straining at the white cotton bra she quickly casts aside as well.

"So beautiful." I barely get the words out before my mouth is on one nipple. I lick and suck the rosy peak, a much better celebration taste than the drink of fire water.

Lia's head rocks back and her face softens in pleasure as I alternate my attention on each side, kissing and smoothing and petting. She slides a hand up my shirt, her palm skating along my stomach, scalding my skin with wanting. I wrestle out of my shirt and hold her against me, our bare skin connecting at last.

My hips jut up from the bed against Lia, desperate for

friction and pressure and she moans, moving with me. Until she freezes.

"Oh. Oh, no. No, no, no." Lia rolls off me and curls into a ball, clutching at her stomach.

"What's wrong?" I smooth back her hair, concerned as she winces, clenching against pain.

Eyes squeezed shut, Lia shakes her head. "I hate this."

I splay a palm across her stomach. "Does this hurt?" Lia nods and I withdraw. "What can I do? How can I help?" I need her to know I'm not afraid of this, not going anywhere. I reach for the comforter and tuck it around her, then pull her onto my lap, cradling her in my arms as Lia begins to weep.

"I'm here, Lia. You've got me."

Her breath is ragged and she purses her lips, eyes closed as she breathes through spasms. "Can you give me a few minutes?" She scrambles from my arms and darts for the bathroom.

I head to the kitchen to get her some ice water and a ginger ale from the fridge. I wait for her in the bedroom and open my arms when she returns, crawling into my embrace. I hold her until she falls asleep, watching her rest in my arms, in awe that she's real and here and mine after so much time.

Eventually I slip from the bed to work on the computer. I figure if Lia can face her demons, I can tackle some electronic paperwork for the farm. I'm grateful that Molly is on her way, glad that I can at least get a few small things off my plate when she gets here, even if it's just farmstand stuff.

Lia's phone starts chirping. I turn off the sound, not wanting to wake her.

A few hours pass and I hear movement from my room. I smile as Lia pads into the kitchen, wrapped in my flannel shirt. I love how she looks in my clothes, how the sleeves are cuffed, the hem hangs nearly to her knees. I know I have all the time in the world to strip her out of it. I'm a patient man.

Lia greets me with a soft kiss on the lips. "Hey, you."

"Feeling better?" I pull her onto my lap, not caring that the small chair creaks under our combined weight. I tuck her under my chin and wrap both arms around her.

# CHAPTER 25
# LIA

I DOUBLE OVER LAUGHING AS ETHAN TUGS MY HAND, tugging me deeper through the woods. Our boots crunch loudly on the gravel path, disrupting birds and squirrels startled by humans invading their haven. But Ethan's boyish enthusiasm proves infectious, and soon I'm rushing alongside him brushing budding branches away from my flushed face.

After yesterday's good news, Ethan has been in a rare great mood, humming to himself while he cared for Baabara this morning and declaring both the strawberry patch and the larger soybean fields to be in excellent condition.

He wrapped up his work early and asked me to join him on an adventure. How could I say no to that? I messaged my boss that I was using half a personal day and paired the news with the grant funding to sweeten the impact.

Ethan and I crash into a clearing together winded but grinning. Red trillium are in bloom alongside beautiful white snowdrops and some yellow flowers whose names

I've forgotten. I spot a soft, checkered blanket spread on the grass, with wicker baskets and incredible aromas of savory food mixed in with the budding field. I gasp softly, hands covering my grin.

"Surprise picnic, just for us." Ethan's ears redden hearing my tiny shrieks of joy. "Thought you'd want some stuff you can actually eat." His brow furrows. "Sorry I'm not much of a cook, but Gran was supervising so it should be alright."

My heart swells realizing no one but Ethan and his grandmother would've noted what foods I must carefully avoid, then taken such pains assembling safe options just to indulge me. I grip his plaid shirt and pull his lips down to mine, my gratitude beyond words and requiring a kiss instead. He was so loving and understanding last night when we were interrupted by stomach pains. I hope above hope that tonight will have a different ending.

When we part I pepper feather-light kisses along Ethan's stubbled jaw, eliciting shivers. I tremble, knowing I can rouse such a reaction from this giant, stoic man. He captures my chin mid-caress, eyes cobalt flame. "Food first," he murmurs, an unspoken second course shimmering in the air. I press closer, anticipating us savoring each other.

Ethan reveals roasted squash with honey, glazed beets, gluten-free bread, and herbed olive oil — Gran's efforts, no doubt. I heap my plate, famished. The afternoon sunshine and Ethan's comforting presence warm me inside and out as we devour this Lia-friendly feast.

Feeling giddy, I spear a chunk of squash and feed it to Ethan, who has hardly eaten anything. He just stares at me, smiling, but he indulges my feeding him with exaggerated moans that make us both giggle. I feel so relaxed with him here, so free, so supported. I bite my lip and feed him another bite of food, and his moan this time doesn't make me laugh.

I'm burning for him, warmed by the sun, feeling brave. I shove the cleared plates to the side and shift closer. His eyes are patient, expectant. "You make me imagine a beautiful future, Ethan Bedd. One that doesn't just include survival." His smile widens and he traces my hand with his thumb. "Will you let me love you again? Give us another chance?"

Ethan stills, processing. The breeze stirs the grass around us. Rather than speak, he slowly frames my face in calloused hands, blue gaze piercing to my churning soul. "I've waited so long for you, Lia. Can hardly believe I'm not just dreaming." His throat bobs. "Promise me this is real — that you're truly here to build a life together. You're my partner now ... in all things?"

My naked need reflected back in Ethan's face tightens my chest. I press my lips to his seeking mouth in answer and confirmation, our kisses kindling sparks, swiftly gaining force as we finally unleash pent up need. We shed our clothes beside the feast, our hunger shifting to physical intimacy. Finally, skin to skin in the sunlight, we sprawl tangled in the grass.

Ethan rolls us so he's on top of me and I wince. Usually, when I'm in a flare, I can't bear the weight of someone above me. But he settles his frame on his forearms and kisses my nose. "Is this okay?" I nod because it's more than just okay. As Ethan licks along my collar bones and down, back to my breasts, I am way, way more than okay.

I let my head roll side to side and bury my fingers in his hair as he licks and sucks along my chest and stomach. Every caress sends shivers and heat clashing through me. I lift my hips to Ethan's, needing the friction and pressure of his hardness. "Oh, it's so, so good," I purr. I actually purr.

Ethan's hands skim my curves, learning the dips and swells of my body until I'm slick and breathless. I arch under him again, delirious as he peels off my panties. I've never been naked outdoors, but here, bare in the sun, I feel more protected than ever.

Ethan kisses my hip, fingers kneading my thighs and spreading me open for him. "So beautiful," he whispers, worshiping my body.

"Ethan, please." I'm not sure what I'm asking for, what I need, but he reaches between my legs to find me wet and wanting. I'm feverish with lust for him. My hips roll and I reach for his length as he shimmies out of his boxers at long last.

He hisses when I wrap a fist around him. "Lia," he pants. "I want you to know I've had a checkup. Clean bill of health." His voice is breathy as I stroke him, loving the long length in my hand, the velvet wrapped around steel with a weeping tip. I use my thumb to spread his precum around the head of his cock and I moan when he groans.

"I'm clear, too," I pant. "In that regard, anyway." I chuckle. "I also can't get pregnant...but I need to talk to you about that eventually...oh!"

Ethan slides a finger inside me and crooks it, beckoning my pleasure as I shout, not caring who or what can hear. "We'll talk all you want. After." Ethan meets my eye and holds my gaze as he strokes me. "Is this still what you like?"

"God yes." I nod furiously as his thumb circles my clit while another long finger strokes inside me. I lose track of what he's doing with his hand as the pleasure spreads, zings and tingles radiating out. Soon, my muscles are clenching and throbbing as I come on his hand, thrashing around in the grass. Ethan's face is pure bliss, satisfied and happy as the waves subside and he positions himself above me.

We join, slick, fevered, crying out for long-denied release and Ethan begins to move. His face contorts with the effort of holding himself above me and concentrating on my body. I watch his abs ripple as he strokes in and out, run my hands along the concave splendor of his ass and enjoy the feel of it contracting beneath my palms.

"Lia, god how I've missed you. Fuck, this feels so damn good."

I have no words, only kisses and thrusts of my hips. There is nothing but this, and when Ethan tilts to one side, bringing a hand to my clit, I rocket off again after just a few firm rubs. He throws his head back and roars, filling me and I can hear both our hearts hammering in sync.

Sometime later, we drift back to earth and Ethan's eyes widen in alarm. "Do you think I'm going to get a sunburn on my ass?"

I burst into laughter as he reaches to pull the picnic blanket around us, the waves of hysteria spreading as our empty dishes and food containers clatter in his haste to cover his butt from the afternoon sun. From somewhere far off, my phone chirps, startling me from where I'd begun to relax and trace shapes in Ethan's chest hair.

I groan, realizing I never switched off my notifications for our romantic adventure. The chirps grow insistent, I stretch an arm toward the sound and retrieve my phone from the grass, squinting to read the screen.

Ethan adjusts his body so his head is blocking my phone from the glare and I gasp, seeing my boss's message on my screen. "Is it bad news?" Ethan asks as I stiffen and try to wriggle from beneath him.

I shake my head and read the message again, holding a hand over my mouth as I look from Ethan to my phone screen and back. "It's a series of excited messages about the grant for the Bedd Fellows Farm."

He smiles. "Well, good. I'm glad they're happy with your work."

I shake my head in disbelief. "My big boss wants me to stay here if I'm willing. Thinks I can help turn around other investments in nearby communities." Stunned disbelief slackens my limbs and I slump over onto Ethan, boneless.

"What are you saying, Lia?"

I press a kiss to his temple and clutch my phone to my chest. "It means I can stay. It means I can stay here with Asher, with … I can stay with *you*, if you'll have me?"

I had to fight for the chance to come here, set up remote operations to turn failing investments around. At the time, I thought maybe I could right a wrong I felt I'd wrought on the Bedd family by shutting Ethan out of my life.

Now the top brass is singing my praises as a creative visionary. But none of it matters, I realize, if Ethan isn't interested in giving me another chance. It's been months of spending time with him. Is it enough? Will he want me here now that I have the flexibility and stability to choose to stay?

Ethan sits up and grabs my face with both hands,

pressing his forehead against mine. I can feel his breath on my face as he says, "Lia, if I had my way, you'd never leave my side ever again." I crush my mouth against his and my anxiety melts away.

We kiss, our bodies communicating our commitment. I can set down roots here, with Ethan.

# CHAPTER 26
# ETHAN

I awaken slowly, a dreamy smile creeping across my face remembering my picnic with Lia, who spent the night with me in my bed.

The coffeemaker gurgles from the kitchen and I slide on my jeans, padding barefoot across the floorboards toward Lia, who stands with her back facing me, wearing only my flannel hanging loose on her beautiful body.

I halt in my tracks, transfixed by the sunlight glowing around her dark hair that glistens. This incredible woman has overcome so much, done so much for my family and me. And now she's mine. *Mine.*

Lia turns, hearing my sharp inhale, mischief sparkling in umber eyes. "See something you like, farm boy?"

I cross over to her quickly, pulling her eager body flush to mine, claiming her teasing lips. We cling together until the teakettle's shrill whistle interrupts my hungry explorations. I release her slowly, heart galloping wildly.

"Coffee or tea?" Lia gestures shyly toward her efforts with morning beverages. My chest constricts, realizing how much I still love her, how I've always loved her. We aren't teens anymore. She's all woman, choosing a second chance with me. I cradle her face between my rough palms, hoping I can summon the right words.

"You being here makes everything perfect. Coffee can wait."

Her cheeks flush a beautiful shade of pink and she presses her lips together, looking up into my eyes. "Ethan, with the meds change....well now that the harsh pills are stopped, technically I might eventually get..."

Lia breaks off, twisting a lock of her hair, teeth worrying a lush lower lip. My pulse quickens realizing the monumental notion looming over our still-new intimacy. I cover her restless hands with mine. "Lia, darling, look at me." I lift her chin slowly and her eyes brim with yearning and worry and tears. I smile. "I'll say it again. You being here is perfect. And if us being together creates a new life, well, then that's perfect, too."

A single tear etches glistening trails down Lia's delicate cheek. Her radiant expression transforms from disbelief into profound relief as I claim her mouth and lift her off the ground. I head for the bedroom with ground-eating strides and set her on the floor by the bed so I can unbutton my shirt, revealing her breasts and the round swell of her belly. I rest a palm there, realizing that someday this belly might swell with my child.

Before my emotions can overwhelm me, she launches herself at me, pushing me flat on my back on the mattress and straddling my body, her wet center rubbing along my already-hard cock. "Oh, god, Lia." I thrust up against her, needing that heat, needing her.

She's quiet and smiling as she adjusts herself to take me into her body in one wet slide. Her hips meet mine and we both look down at the place where we're connected. I place her hand on my heart. "I'm yours, Lia. I've always been yours."

"And I'm yours, Ethan. Forever." Lia begins to rock and sway, I lie back, watching the incredible show. She slides a hand down her own chest and the sight has me harder than ever. When her hand reaches her cleft, she begins to moan and touch herself. My breath comes in pants as she takes what she needs, bringing me along with her for the best ride of my life.

"Yes, Lia. Show me what you need."

"You always give me exactly what I need," she pants, rocking and grinding, grunting in effort until her head snaps back and I feel her pulsing around me. She shudders above me and moves a few more times before I feel the white-hot burst of pleasure building from the base of my spine.

I clasp her hips, fingers digging into her soft flesh, and I thrust up and spill into her, hot and hard.

Lia collapses onto my chest and I run my fingers lazily through her hair, both of us working to slow our hearts and breath. We are nearly asleep, sticky and warm, when my front door bursts open with a horrifying sound.

Through the open bedroom door, I see Baabara clop into my house, bleating, dragging a leash behind her and splashing clots of mud along my floor. "Baabara, what the hell?"

I flail around the room in search of my pants, lunging out of bed to chase her. I need to grab the sheep before she destroys my entire house. Before I even have my pants pulled on, she sticks a head into the bedroom, appears to assess the situation, and bleats twice before trotting back out the door.

Lia is doubled over in hysterics as I hop around, trying to get my feet into some shoes so I can chase Baabara down. I glance over my shoulder at my … at my Lia, still laughing and gorgeously disheveled. "Be here when I get back," I bark at her. Her peals of laughter follow me as I bolt after the damn sheep.

# CHAPTER 27
# ETHAN

THE FARM IS TRANSFORMING SLOWLY AND YET MUCH MORE rapidly than I'd like. Six weeks pass without further incident–either from Baabara or Lia's immune system. I've been on edge about the strawberry harvest and distracting myself trying to read up about Lia's condition. She keeps telling me to keep my eyes on my own paper.

It's certainly easier for me to see to the soybean seeds than it is to fuss over the fickle berry crop, but Gran assures me the fruit is fine. All I can say is that it had better be. We're about to be open for business.

We transformed the pole barn from tractor storage facility to strawberry central, and today is what Lia calls our soft opening. From my perspective, there's nothing soft about it...it's hard making all these changes. But maybe that just means the reward will be sweeter, this time.

I left Lia in our bed before dawn and hurried to check the soybean crop before getting my marching orders from Colleen, Molly, and Gran. I crest the hill and see my girl up in the barn with my family, and I just know that everything is as it should be. Well, should is a strong word. Nobody will ever convince me we need strawberry-scented candles or -flavored milk, but Molly says these kinds of things sell like wild. Alex was definitely not consulted with the choice to market the strawberry-flavored milk, and he was steaming mad when Gran told him he had to shut up and try the idea.

Not gonna lie, I take comfort knowing I'm not the only Bedd sibling feeling the growing pains of this financial crisis. Before we officially open our gates, I string bistro lights along the eaves, and Molly directs vendors through their paces, ticking items off a lengthy list while Lia follows, obviously delighted.

I watch as Lia shakes hands with soap makers and jam purveyors, conveying infectious excitement. My chest puffs proudly at the results of Lia's vision. Even as I begin to suspect the barn is a little tight for all the things we're trying to do here to turn a profit.

Molly is clearly thriving and capable, although for some reason my brother keeps watching her from where he leans against the doorframe like he thinks she's gonna make a run for it. I meet his eye and climb down the ladder, making my way over to him.

I haven't called Alex yet. I said I would, but things have been too busy. "I owe you a phone call. We should talk."

Alex heaves a sigh, hands in his pockets. "Sure."

He says it in the tone of voice that tells me he doesn't believe me. "What is that supposed to mean?"

He shrugs, the muscle in his jaw popping. "It's been months since you said that.."

If I didn't know any better, I'd think my brother was

*offended.* I gesture around. "Well, we've got shit going on right now."

Alex looks away, and we're both quiet for a moment. I glance in the direction he's looking and see Lia, who is again wearing my shirt, but she has it knotted at her waist over a pair of form-hugging jeans. She looks right at home here with my family, and I intend to keep it that way. "She staying, then?" He gestures at Lia with one thumb, I nod. His lips tip up briefly in a ghost of a smile. "Good. Always thought you two were good together."

Molly walks toward us. Alex stiffens even more than normal, a frown sliding back in place. She taps a clipboard and says, "We are as ready as we'll ever be, boss."

I wave a hand at her. "I told you not to call me that. I think Lia's the one really in charge. Or maybe Gran, since she's the one who hired you."

She shakes her head. "Well, if we're going by who is actually paying me..." Molly grins at Alex and pokes at the Udderly Creamy Farm polo my brother wears. He frowns even deeper. "Boss," she says with a lilting tease.

Technically, we're bartering with Molly, giving her a place to park her van in exchange for work. Since we aren't going to have as much for Molly to do on weekdays, Gran sent her over to interview with Alex, who had no idea she was also working here with us. He's been short someone to run his own farm stand since the last cashier left a few weeks ago. Let's just say my brother isn't the best person to work directly with customers. I can say that because I'm not, either.

Alex tips his chin at Molly, then glances over at me. "I've got work to do back at the farm. Good luck today."

My brother spins on his heel and leaves, his dog

emerging from Baabara's house and following him into his truck.

"You excited for your first day at the farm stand next Thursday?" Lia asks Molly.

Our temp squeals and claps her hands together, bouncing on her toes. "So excited."

Molly practically skips away, and Lia and I watch her go.

"Oil and water, those two." I comment.

Lia wraps an arm around my waist and fits herself against my side. "You think it's going to be a problem?"

"Not sure." I plant a kiss on top of her head. "But we'll worry about it after the weekend, right?"

# CHAPTER 28
# LIA

I SMOOTH FLYAWAY HAIRS, SECURING THEM INTO MY BRAID while anxiety gnaws my empty stomach. Today's a big day for so many reasons. The Bedd family's future hinges on the success of the strawberry harvest and today's the first day the public can come pick their own berries. But it's also the first of my infusions with Dr. Sanchez at the Climax hospital.

I was worried about being away from the farm for so long on an important day, but Ethan assured me they have things under control, so I took the first available appointment after my blood draw.

My reflection is interrupted by a sharp rap at the bedroom door. Before I respond, Gran herself breezes in, toting a clothing box and wearing an uncharacteristically timid expression belying her usual confidence. She perches gingerly on the bedspread, patting a hand beside her.

I sit and notice that she's got a lumpy package with her. "I have something for you, Lia." Her voice quavers slightly. She pats the wrapping. "I started making this for you all those years back when my Ethan was so lovesick.

Wanted you to have it when you left for school and ... well ..." Her eyes squeeze shut, as if blotting out the pain of those years. I know it was hard for all of us.

My own throat constricts, recalling the confused panic severing soul-deep connections in brutal self-protection.

Gran clucks dismissively as if scolding her own emotions into check. "What matters is you're here now, showing this obstinate family how to grow again. Can't change what wilted on tough seasons past, but you're helping us tend new sprouts within reach." Her palm squeezes firmer, voice growing thick. "Anyhow, wanted you to have what I made special, back when. Few changes to the pattern for your medical particulars."

She gestures and I open the package, revealing a berry-red knitted sweater, made from the softest merino wool. I gasp, running my fingers along the expertly stitched material. "Ethel! It's incredible."

She smiles. "That's Baabara's finest. I haven't done that dye batch since. Might do it again this summer, though. After the berry success." We both run our hands along the gift, pausing midway down each sleeve, where I see Gran has made small flaps held shut with beautiful wooden buttons.

"Are these for my IV lines?" Tears well in my eyes and I'm grateful for once when I hear the telltale sign of Baabara making her way uninvited into the cabin.

"Thought you could keep it on and stay warm and the nurses could access your veins that way." Gran coos and snaps her fingers at the sheep, who trots into the bedroom and nuzzles Gran's lap.

I reach between the sheep's ears, scratching. "Thank you, too, Baabara. This is the most wonderful wool!" My eyes water helplessly at Baabara and Gran's expansive efforts welcoming me into the family and the farm's legacy so unconditionally.

Wordlessly I stand and fiercely wrap both arms around her sturdy shoulders. "It's absolutely perfect. Thank you so much."

Gran kisses my cheek and pats my shoulder. "It was always my pleasure, Lia. Now. You coming back to us after you wear it today?" I nod, easing into the cardigan and finding it fits me perfectly.

Gran's crinkled features soften into a poignant smile, squeezing my wrist tightly. "I'm holding you to that, Miss Thorne."

Right on cue, Asher's SUV rumbles up the drive. I inhale deeply, centering my thoughts. Obviously, I don't like the vulnerability of a chronic illness, but I feel the promise of today's treatment. This is the beginning of a conversation between Dr. Sanchez and me, and I'm proud I'm able to achieve this while also keeping the job I went to school to learn. I make my way onto the porch, Baabara at my heels.

Ethan's walking toward me and Baabara bleats her excitement at seeing him. "You taking an escort to Climax?" Dry wit dances in his cobalt eyes as he pets the sheep and nudges her toward Asher's car.

I swat Ethan's chest playfully as he guffaws, escaping my ineffective swipe. We've built a natural, lighthearted intimacy in such a short time, despite the lonely years we spent apart. I vow silently never to go there again. There's no need when Ethan and I trust each other so deeply now as adults. Asher leans out his open window, hollering impatience, as Baabara nudges my thigh insistently.

Behind us, car engines begin to signal the start of the Bedd Family festivities.

With a swift kiss and tighter hug, I pull away from Ethan, heading toward a new way of life. Asher is grouchier than usual on the brief ride, complaining about some new person who moved onto the abandoned property on the other side of our house. The last owners used to produce maple syrup there, but the land has been vacant at least since I left town.

I smile at his grumblings and kiss his cheek when he drops me at the door of the clinic. I told him I want to go in alone and I wave as he drives off. Clutching my new sweater tightly around my shoulders, I head inside.

Before long I'm seated comfortably in a padded chair, an audiobook Colleen recommended in my ear buds. I sigh contentedly as the meds drip slowly over the next hour.

Asher drops me back at Bedd Fellows Farm amid a wild frenzy of screaming kids and sunshine. I am immediately thrust into action mode amidst the vendor stands in the barn. The smells of elaborate spinach quiches with squash blossoms mix with elderflower iced tea and lavender honey cakes. The rich aromas set my empty stomach rumbling and I wonder, as I field questions, what I could eat that would feel good.

I pass Colleen debriefing community volunteers who spent the day monitoring berry picking etiquette. Molly's happily collecting money, smile already bright enough to blind visitors. Her confidence and attention to detail confirm Gran's astute talent scouting. It's clearly been an amazing day on the farm.

Sweeping string lights cast a festive glow as golden hour dapples the landscape and I spy Gran off to the side, deep in conversation with Latonya from the Lick Your Fork diner. Both women laugh loud and heartily as I approach and I smile, accepting hugs from both of them. "You feeling okay, sugar?" Latonya eyes me and I bite my lip.

"I would love something to eat if I can find something safe…"

Latonya and Gran trade glances and LT claps her hands. "I have just the thing!" She steers me past Alex Bedd, deep in conversation with Diego and Chen from town. At the end of the row of vendors, Latonya gestures toward a stand boasting allergen-friendly foods. I gasp, spying gluten free muffins. My mouth waters at the sight of a berry jam parfait with grain-free coconut yogurt.

"This is perfect!" I barely squeak out my thanks before I start inhaling the delicacy, nodding and moaning in appreciation as Latonya re-introduces me to the town elders. My head swims, not with dizziness from my infusion but from pride and joy at the beautiful gathering that came from such a tragedy for the Bedd family.

I watch Ethan staring at young children sticky with strawberry juice. No spreadsheets can accurately capture the wealth here today, with half the town frolicking in the berry rows. This little soybean farm embraced change when they needed to, and I treasure the opportunity to be here to see its success.

Soon enough I am pulled back toward pressing realities, finding Alex and Ethan assessing register receipts and reviewing supplier invoices for the market. I spy Samuel and Colleen approaching them and I make my way toward the Bedd siblings.

I recall with perfect clarity the soaring hope Ethan's eyes shone with just this morning. As the crowds disperse and the vendors pack up for the day, I can tell the Bedd family is eager to hear the final tally.

I gesture for Molly to hand over her cash and settle in with my laptop at one of the picnic tables beneath the twinkle lights. The Bedd family huddles nearby and I hear them making small talk, sipping tea, knowing their future depends on the outcome.

When I glance up, Ethan meets my eye immediately and walks to my side. I rub his taut forearm and sigh. "Today was incredible, Ethan. We made so much more revenue than we hoped."

He seems to sag in relief and, seeing that, his family jumps to their feet. I clench my teeth and gesture at the papers. "We always knew it wasn't going to be enough, though. You're still in a really precarious place."

Alex frowns. "What's that supposed to mean? Foreclosure, still?"

I shake my head. "Not imminently, no. Today was a very, very good season opener. The grant money paired with the harvest revenue should more than cover your back payments and start to chip away at the interest a bit. But, you all knew the principle was extremely high…"

Ethan nods. "We knew. But I thought this would be enough going forward. The strawberries and having all the vendors here this spring…" Under the dim lights I can see creases and lines around his face. I hold my breath, quickly calculating how long our cushion buys before the

Bedds face harsh choices again. This isn't the time to suggest clever investments or additional loans.

Ethan draws me to his chest, presses his lips sweetly to my temple. I exhale, relaxing into the anchor of his embrace. We are in this together.

I look him in the eye. "We need to regroup. Maybe restructure the business. There isn't enough space here to do what we need."

Ethan nods. Gran sighs. Samuel kicks a table. I notice Alex stroking his chin, thoughtful. I smile at him. "Let's all plan to meet again and discuss some options. We've got another week of peak strawberry madness and then we can debrief."

Gran and Colleen make their way to the house. Molly and Alex walk off towards her van, Molly chattering away while Alex looks down at her, brows furrowed in concentration. I glance at Ethan, surprised to see his brother wandering off in the dark with his employee.

"You don't think…" I start.

"What?"

I shake my head. Based on the way Molly was with customers today, she might be able charm her way into almost anyone's heart. But Alex would be a challenge. Though close in age to Ethan, Alex always seemed lonely to me. Maybe I should butt out and see what Molly does.

"Nevermind. Let's go to bed, Ethan. We've got a long day tomorrow."

He nods again and tugs me with him. Hand in hand, we walk toward the welcoming glow of the light from Ethan's cabin. Our cabin? As he plants a kiss on my neck, I feel confident in the latter description. At the door I lift our joined hands and tenderly kiss Ethan's scratched knuckles. We cross the threshold into our sanctuary. Into our home.

Want to find out what's next for Bedd Fellows Farm? The fun continues in Butter You Up by Liz Alden, where grumpy dairy farmer Alex falls for sunshiney #vanlifer Molly. Plus, goats and an a-derp-able farm dog!

Want more Ethan and Lia? My newsletter subscribers get an exclusive epilogue of their happily ever after. Visit LaineyDavis.com to sign up.

# FARM TO FORKING SERIES

Bedd Fellows Farm is in trouble. Grandad bequeathed the five Bedd siblings a heap of debt, along with a troublesome sheep, and they're all too stubborn to accept the help they need to dig their way out of the compost pile.

Join authors Lainey Davis, Liz Alden, Karen Grey, Erin Mallon, and Ember Leigh as they share un-baa-lievable tales of love, laughter, and sexy shenanigans, all set in the bucolic fictional town of Fork Lick, New York.

Meddling grandmas, nosy neighbors, and boinking abound in these steamy romantic comedies:

**Since You've Bean Gone** by Lainey Davis

**Butter You Up** by Liz Alden

**For Fork's Sake** by Karen Grey

**Bringing Home the Bacon** by Erin Mallon

**A Fork in the Road** by Ember Leigh

# MORE FROM THE AUTHORS

Catch up with the Bedds' neighbors in the Planted and Plowed series by **Lainey Davis**. Asher Thorne is the hero of Sappy Go Lucky.

Take your romcoms with a side of wanderlust. Kit gets his own story in the upcoming Anywhere But Here series by **Liz Alden**. In the meantime, check out Aged Like Fine Wine, where four best friends explore Europe and love after forty!

Stayed tuned for a new small town romcom series coming soon from **Karen Grey**, set down the road from Fork Lick! In the meantime, check out her nostalgic romance at karengrey.com.

As a girl with four brothers, Colleen Bedd knows what it's like to be "one of the guys." For more strong heroines who aren't afraid to go head-to-head with their fellas, dive into The Natural History Series by **Erin Mallon**.

Jackson's leading lady hails from Bayshore, a small, lakeside Ohio town that sets the stage for **Ember's** other rom-coms. Visit Bayshore now to meet the Daly brothers, and to get ready for the next series launching soon.

# ACKNOWLEDGMENTS

I need to thank my co-collaborators for their work in helping me bring this book to life. What a joy it has been to brainstorm this ridiculous town and this banana-pants family! It has been a true delight and a growth opportunity to work with each of you.

I'd also like to thank Evie Troutman and Doug Nelson for sharing allllll the dirty details about life with Crohn's disease. I learned more about poop researching this book than I ever imagined, and I appreciate them for keeping it real with me. I really hope Lia's story with Crohn's feels authentic. I know that a lot of people live with tricky bowel conditions and my goal was to show what happily ever after can look like for those folks.

Thank you as well to Elizabeth Perry, Melissa Wiesner, Liz Lincoln and Sara Whitney for your help with the plot and to Becky at Bookcase Media for the edit. My intern, Felicia Perez, has been an incredible support this year.

And you, readers, have been a true bumper crop. You are blue ribbon fans and I cannot wait to hear what you think about Ethan and Lia. Thank you for following me all the way to a fictional small town and back again.